Bob Moats

I0567415

Network
Murders

By Bob Moats

Network Murders

For information and address:
Magic 1 Productions
P.O. Box 524, Fraser MI 48026-0524
Website: http://murdernovels.com
Cover by Bob Moats

Bob Moats

Other Jim Richards series books by Bob Moats

For a preview or to purchase a book, go to
http://murdernovels.com

What a few people are saying about the Murder Novels by Bob Moats

Mr. Moats, I just got your novel "Classmate Murders" and have to let you know, I read it in one evening. That is the first book I have ever done that with. That was the most enjoyable book I have ever read. I just started reading e-books, and reading again, after getting my wife a Kindle. This book was my 12th, and the best. I just got Las Vegas Showgirls to (read) tomorrow evening. ☺. I look forward to reading many of your books in this series. I have been searching for an author and books that were fun, entertaining reads. Your books are just the ticket.

Regards, A new fan, Bill from South Carolina

****

Hi Bob, I just had to write you... Last week I purchased a Nook Soft Touch e-reader. I was downloading free e-books and downloaded "Classmate Murders" from Barnes & Noble. I read it that night and enjoyed it so much that I went to search for the next one (as listed at end of the book). Read it and searched again. After reading the second one, I did a search from my e-reader for you and bought ALL of the books. So in the last week I have read all of the Jim Richards books. Finished the last one early this morning. I only read at night 10-6 when my neighbor is asleep. As I read the books I sometimes laughed and sometimes cried. I could relate to Jim as we are both in the 60s. I liked how "Jim" refers to previous murders in each book. That is great for anyone who has not read the books in order and also as fast as I did. Anyway, I just had to write and tell you how much I enjoyed the books.

Nancie S.

****

Another very nice comment submitted through my website from a person named Micki P.:

"I recently was given a kindle for my 60th birthday. The first book I downloaded was the Classmate Murders and have now read every one of the them. Today I started on the Fatal Rejection series. Thank you for the wonderful ride with Jim and Penny and all the rest of the troop. I have laughed and giggled thru the stories, my poor family gave me the strangest looks! Now I really want a little Yorkie!! Fatal Rejection so far is another great read! I will be looking out for more of Jim Richards and since you are my #1 Author, anything of yours I can find."

****

Received a feedback form reply on my website from a Cassy B. Here's what she said:

"Well, I just finished all 22 of your novels. I certainly hope you are hard at work at your laptop. I haven't run straight through a series since John D. MacDonald's Travis McGee series. I thoroughly enjoy your characters, the plot twists and the humor in all your stories. Keep them coming!"

Extra special thanks to:

My gratitude to Sally Berneathy who edited this book and is editing some of my other books. If you need an editor for your work go to http://sallyberneathy.com for more info.

Thank you for purchasing this book. I hope you enjoy it as much as I enjoyed writing it for my faithful readers. Please feel free to email me to tell me what you thought about my stories. I love hearing from the readers. I can be reached at murdernovels@bobmoats.com thanks again!

Network Murders by Bob Moats

Prologue

Percy Isham sat at his desk poring over the new season's television schedule, trying to balance the shows. There were formulas for what shows followed another and at what times of the day. He was studying the daytime lineup and trying to decide where to balance the second run shows around the new talk show. Well, Penny Wickens' talk show was not new to this network. Three years ago, they had her show running until that serial killer started to murder her guests. Her show was pulled off the air, but the killer threatened to murder more people if she wasn't put back on. They yielded to his demands and the situation went bad until that private eye and his buddies managed to stop the killer.

However, Penny Wickens used her contractual option to leave her show. She was not happy with the way the network handled the situation and they lost a ratings gold mine. Now they got her back, and it was going to be a big celebration when her show premiered next week. They spent a lot of money on advertisements to promote the show. This time it was from Las Vegas, another ratings winner.

Network Murders

They wanted the show to go on earlier but Wickens and her husband needed a couple weeks to take a vacation before getting back into it. She had now returned to Vegas and they had everything ready for her debut.

Isham sat in his office in Vegas, since he was the west coast head of programming. He opted to leave LA and settle in Vegas for many reasons. One was gambling, another was celebrities for the pickings to put in his shows.

It was nine in the evening. He liked to work late then go gambling. He finished his changes in the lineup and was happy with his decisions. The casinos awaited him and the bevy of women who knew him and wanted to bed the man who could put them on TV. Not that he really could get them a shot on television, but he led them to believe that.

He put everything safely away and went to the door of his office. He was alone in the building, the way he liked it. Less headaches dealing with people. He opened the door and was confronted by a dark figure in the outer room. He was startled.

"How did you get in here and who are you?" he asked.

The figure didn't respond, but came forward to the man. In the light of Isham's office he could see the stranger's face clearly.

"What the hell are you doing in here? I told you that I was not going to have any further dealings with you. I'm calling the police if you don't leave right now," Isham said.

It was the last words Percy Isham would ever speak as the figure brought up a gun and fired at the man.

*

Chapter 1

We spent another week of our vacation visiting with Dave and Sarah in Brinnon, Washington. It was pleasant, fun and we even got to explore Seattle with them. But we had to be back to Vegas to get ready for Penny's triumphant return to network television.

We drove back and arrived a day later after staying again at the RV park from hell. Unfortunately there were no children on our return. Penny was sad and I had to collect the wood myself to have a fire.

We drove into Vegas and went straight to our home. Willy made good use of the front lawn. I would have to clean it up later or leave it as fertilizer. But first I wanted to unpack the van.

As I was unloading, I saw a car driving up. It was Trapper. He pulled in and parked.

"How did you know we were back?" I asked when he came up to me.

"I have my sources," he said with a sly grin. "How was the vacation?"

"It was very relaxing. We got to see a good portion of Seattle and all around Brinnon. Nice little town and good, friendly people."

"I heard that the guy who kidnapped Penny and Sarah is getting a long sentence and time in Gitmo. They are classifying him as a terrorist now. They said the drug he was going to push was a biological weapon. So they can bypass the regular channels of jurisprudence. The company that was developing the drug is under investigation also."

"I like the way they think. How's the office doing?"

"Buck is moping around since he put Mac in charge of the security. You need to get him something to do. Earl is out on a case of theft in one of the casinos. Petty theft, if you must know. Earl is not happy, but willing to take on the case. Lacey hasn't committed any murders yet, but she's threatening to murder Mac if he doesn't get his reports done on time. You're going to be threatened also for the same crime."

"Hey, I've been gone. I don't have any cases to report. You're just passing the buck," I said.

"Well, you deal with her. I'm going to take a few days off and reconnect with Sam. We've been drifting apart lately."

"You just couldn't hook up with that bimbo from the strip club, what was her name, Peaches LaFargo?"

"Peaches LaFarge. And she missed her opportunity when she didn't go out with me. The cop she hooked up with is a dipwad. But I'm not suffering," he said with a laugh.

"Sure, you got your woman. Now don't mess it up. Sam is a good woman despite her shady activities and past," I said.

"The way I like them, loose and dangerous. When's Penny's show start?"

"Monday is the first taping. The network has been promoting the hell out of it. We even saw the commercials up in Brinnon."

"So did you bond with this country sheriff?" Trapper asked, with a grin.

"He's a decent guy and I wouldn't mind him working with us. He seems ready for a change."

"We already have enough men now who can't find enough cases to investigate. One more person and we would be past our limit."

"I know, it's just that Dave and his wife are good people. I wouldn't mind them being around."

"Whatever, I have to go pick up Sam. We're going over to Kingman to get away from Vegas."

Network Murders

"Why are you going to Arizona and not towards California? Los Angeles isn't that far," I said.

"We want to get away from the big cities. Kingman is just fine with us," he said.

"Well, have a good time. I'll be thinking of you as Lacey bugs me about your reports."

"Just tell her I'll get to them when I get back," he said with a grin and went back to his car. He still didn't like saying good-bye.

I finished unloading the van. All of Penny's store bought packages were put in the spare bedroom so she could sort them out. Willy was at my heels as I put the last of the camping gear away. I took him out for a run and a dump.

I was in the front yard looking out at the strip in the distance. It wasn't lit up yet but still looked beautiful. Willy yipped at me and I took him back in the house.

Penny was in the kitchen making a sandwich for her and, surprisingly, one for me.

"Thank you," I said as she handed it to me.

"I saw you talking to Will out front. What did he want?"

"Nothing much, just welcoming us back. He's going off with Sam to Kingman for a couple days."

"Doesn't anyone work in your business? Seems Earl and Will take a lot of time going off with their girlfriends. You're almost as bad, always off with Deacon and Lynn chasing criminals."

"We have enough work to keep us busy. The money is still coming in. Mostly from the security guard end of it. Buck's men are keeping us from welfare." I laughed. "If you don't need me, I'm going to the office to see what's left of the business."

"Go ahead. Willy and I will be busy sorting my new clothes. I need to look good for my return to national television."

I gave her a kiss and went out to my Crown Vic. It had sat in the garage for way too long. It needed to be driven. I went to the office and parked in the back. I figured I'd go in the back door just to ring the cowbell for Lacey.

The door was locked, which surprised me. I dug my key out and went in. The bell rang for my arrival and I waved to the camera above me. I was waiting to hear Lacey yell something to me. She didn't.

I went by Earl's office. It was empty. I guess he was out chasing petty thieves. I knew Trapper's office would be vacant so just went by it. I stopped at Buck's door and looked in. Mac was sitting behind the desk looking frazzled.

"Mac, is everything okay?" I asked.

He looked startled and then caught a breath. "I'm fine, it's just all the paperwork to keep track of all the guards. I don't know how Buck managed."

"Where is Buck?" I asked.

"He went out to get Maria and they're going to lunch. Don't get me wrong, I like this job. But you have to find something for Buck to do or he'll be right back in this seat."

"What about bodyguard jobs? Isn't there some celebrity he could watch?"

"We have a couple businessmen from Japan who want to have guards with them. And one minor ranked rapper in town who wants us to watch him because of threats against him. Those guys are crazy."

"I'll see what I can find for Buck. He likes keeping busy. With you in charge now, he's just feeling lost. Have him see me when he gets back."

"I will, thanks," Mac said and went back to his paperwork.

I went to the dreaded main lobby where Lacey prowled. I went through the glass doors and to the counter. Lacey looked at me and smiled. I was stunned.

"So how was your trip?" she asked nicely.

I was apprehensive but answered, "Very nice, thank you. How are you feeling?"

"I'm great. Mac is close by and I like that. I always worried when he was out in some bad area guarding shady characters."

"Now he's in the office working with shady characters. Any messages for me while I was gone?"

"Nope. I would have emailed them to you if you had any. Is Penny ready for the big time again?"

"Oh yeah. She bought a ton of clothing on our trip and is trying to decide what to wear on her first show."

"First impressions are important. It's been over three years since she did a national show. I'd be surprised if she's not nervous."

"Penny never shows nervousness or fear. She worries me sometimes that she'll explode one day."

"I'm sure she'll be fine. Being a talk show host is what she's done for years. I don't think she'll explode."

"Yeah, well, if you don't hear from me for a few days, send Lynn and Deacon to our house. They may find me floating in the pool face down," I said with a smile.

*

Chapter 2

I sat in my office going over the reports of the last month. They showed what we had accomplished in investigations and the fees we charged. This month was slow but we made enough to pay everyone and take care of the utilities. I would hate to come into the office and find the electricity was shut off.

The reports also included the security side of the business, which amounted to almost seventy percent of our income. I was glad that when we first came here Buck wanted to start a security guard service. I personally didn't have to worry about income. My books were selling well and Penny was making good money at her job. We kept our money separate, but, if needed, we pooled it.

I knew that Earl had money stashed from his days in the CIA, conquering countries and plundering foreign banks. Trapper had a good pension from his years on the police force, so he was covered. Buck had a pension from the auto company he worked for, so he would survive. Now Lacey, Mac and Tracey had nothing other than this job. I had to be sure they were taken care of.

I heard the glass doors from the lobby open and close. Someone was approaching my office. It was Buck.

"Hey, big guy, how's it going?" I asked.

Bob Moats

Buck came in and plopped down on my client chair. He sat back and smiled that walrus smile I enjoyed seeing.

"I'm good, but a little bored. Since I turned over the responsibilities to Mac, I haven't had much to do," he replied.

"Do you feel like doing your own investigations?"

"I know I could, but I'm not licensed as an investigator."

"Well, since you work for us I'm sure we can get you licensed. Want to do that?"

"Sure, I'm game. When do we start?" Buck asked, sounding excited. I didn't blame him. I was excited when I got my license.

"I need to talk to Deacon and Lynn and see if I can get their help starting this. Just be patient and it will happen," I said.

"Thanks, buddy. I appreciate it," he replied.

We sat talking about my vacation and adventures in Washington State. Then Buck stood.

"Let me know what I have to do to start. I'd like to get working on this."

We finished up and he left. I sat back and thought about calling Lynn and Deacon. I hadn't talked to them in a while. I hadn't been back long enough to bother them. I reached for my phone and called their home. I had a

17

feeling they were there with the baby. About three rings later, Lynn answered.

"I hope you don't need help with a case, Richards," Lynn said. It sounded good to hear her voice again.

"Well, I do need a small favor. I need to get Buck licensed as a P.I. Can you help on that?"

"Going to turn him loose on Vegas?" she said with a laugh.

"I need to give him something to do since he gave up his job as boss for the guards."

"Okay, have him call me this week and I'll talk to the right people. He's worked for your firm so he qualifies. Now, how was your vacation?"

"Well, other than what you saw when we invaded Vegas, and thank you for your help, the vacation was good. We had a nice time out with the sheriff and his wife. Since you're part of the Clark County Sheriff's Department, do you know how hard it is to get in?"

"Is your new friend interested in moving to Sin City? Don't they have enough big time crime up there?"

"Just a thought. Dave asked about it."

"You know, Jim, you're going to run out of favors from me, but I could see what it would take to get him hired," Lynn said with a laugh.

"Don't rush. I'm not sure if they would want to move. But keep it on the back burner for now. Penny and I got to climb the Space Needle in Seattle. She didn't even try to push me off."

Lynn laughed loudly. "Now you've been high in two places. Was it worse than the Stratosphere here?"

"I think the Stratosphere is higher, but I wasn't going to measure it. Other than that it was a good trip. Now we have to get Penny ready to go national again with her show. She's excited, but I think apprehensive, too," I said.

"Why?" Lynn asked.

"I don't know. She seems a bit reluctant to get back into that grind. Her talk show here in Vegas has no pressure to entertain, but the thought of trying to keep the ratings up for the national show may get to her."

"She's a trouper. I'm sure she'll be all right once she gets into the swing of it."

"I know that. She just needs to know. I'll be there to boost her on, and she has her crew to help. Her producer, Gordy, will spur her on. His butt is on the line for this to go well also."

"See if you can get us in to her opening show. We can give her encouragement."

"I'll do that, thanks. How's the baby doing?"

"Don't ask. She's great but not sleeping well at night. Deacon and I take turns with her, but it's hard. I thought dealing with crime was nerve wracking. Babies can be plain frustrating," she said.

"Are you going back to crime fighting?"

"I may take a leave for a while until the baby is old enough to stay with a sitter. Just a year maybe. Deacon is ready to get back to work, so I may chase him out soon. He's a bigger baby than the baby."

We talked a little more and then finished. I sat back thinking about everything that was going on around me. My life was definitely never dull.

I went out to the lobby and stood at the counter. Lacey was busy in a drawer of her desk when she saw me and jumped with a yelp.

"Damn, you haven't done that in a while. It sort of felt good," she said, with a big smile.

"Glad to oblige. I'm going back home to help Penny decide what to wear for her big premier Monday. If you need me, call. Buck is in his office so you and Tracey won't be alone. Is Tracey out in the outer lobby?"

"Yep, she's out there. She never complains about being alone."

"She's probably reading. I'll have to get her a small TV to watch. So I'll be back later, maybe."

"I won't hold my breath," she said sarcastically.

Now that was the Lacey I remembered. Good to see she hadn't lost that touch. I left and went to my car just as Earl was pulling in. I waited until he came over.

"So how did your petty theft case go?" I asked.

"It was a petty crime and a petty waste of time. The casino could have handled it but it was a tourist staying there that hired me. She wanted a real detective to handle the case as she said. I made sure to charge her good." He grinned and then asked, "Did you survive being away from us?"

"I had a great time, but missed everyone. Now that I'm back, I think I may take another vacation."

Earl laughed and said he was going to turn in his report to Lacey and go take Paula out for dinner. He went in and I got in my car and drove out. I decided to take a short drive up the strip just to look at the wonder of it all. I enjoyed taking a ride by the casinos and the tons of people visiting. It was like a big Disneyland for adults.

I headed back and got to the house, pulling into the garage. I went in and it was quiet. I thought Penny might be out in the pool, although it was fairly cold out now that we were in the fall of the year. Vegas wasn't like Michigan for weather, but it still would get cold out here.

I headed back to the spare bedroom and found Penny and Willy asleep on the bed with her new clothes spread around her. I stood at the door, smiling.

I gently woke her and she stretched. "Hey, sweetie, what time is it?" she asked.

21

Network Murders

I looked at my watch and said, "Just after three. Did you pass out?" Willy was coming to life and stood up on the bed. I picked him up and said, "Feel like going out for something to eat?"

"Or I could cook something," she said with an evil smile.

"I think we need to go see Angelo and Carol." I turned and went out, followed by my wife.

"So is the office still running smoothly without you?" she asked behind me.

"Of course it is. It's a well-oiled machine, capable of running smoothly without me. Lacey keeps every one grounded. I even got to scare her."

"You are so cruel. I'm hungry, so step it up," she demanded.

We drove out to Mama Mia, Angelo's restaurant, and parked. We entered and Angelo was by the front counter.

"Mr. and Mrs. R, good to see you. Are you back from your vacation now?"

"We are and we are also hungry. Is Carol working today?"

"Yes, your daughter is busy working hard. She's a real gem to have in my kitchen. Everyone loves the food she prepares. Do you want to see her?"

"Seat us first, then send her out," I said.

"Right this way," he said. "My best table for my good friends."

*

Chapter 3

Angelo sat us at the table and said, "I have a special announcement to tell you, but first you need to eat. Do you want to see your daughter?"

"Please, send her to us if she's not too busy." I said.

"I'll do that, but don't leave before I give you my good news." Angelo beamed and went off to the kitchen.

"I wonder what he has to tell us," Penny said.

"It must be important to him. I hope it's good news," I said.

Carol came up to our table and greeted us. "Are you back from your vacation now?"

"Yep, it was good, too. We'll give you the details later. Now how are you?"

"I'm fine. Busy and enjoying it. I have a special meal to prepare for you, so be ready," she said. We talked a little more then she went back to the kitchen.

Network Murders

I could see Angelo was moving around the dining room, looking happy. I hoped he had something good to tell us.

Shortly after, our food came and we ate. It was good, something Italian and probably unpronounceable. We finished and our waitress took away our plates, giving them to the busboy. I asked her to send Angelo over.

Angelo came to our table and I said, "I know you're busy, but please sit."

He did, and was grinning. I asked, "What do you have on your devious little mind?"

He sat back and then said, "I have a new lady friend. She's someone who is in the restaurant equipment business. I met her through the restaurant. She was trying to sell me new kitchen equipment, which I already have. She confessed to me that she wanted to meet me, so she made up the sales pitch. I hate to admit it but I had her checked out. She's legit and a looker. I'm not great looking so I was suspicious, but she admitted that she was impressed by my love of this restaurant."

"Well, Angelo, that's great," Penny said. "Is she from Vegas?"

"Yeah, she works in the city and is coming in this week for a special dinner. I want to invite you two to join us. You are the closest I have to family here in Vegas, so I want to show you off," he said with a grin.

"Angelo, we'd be honored. Let us know when and we'll clear our schedule. What's her name?" I asked.

"Sophia. She's Italian, and she's a looker. Oh, I already said that," he said with a boyish smile.

"I'm sure she is, my friend. Let us know when and we'll be here," I said.

"Thanks, Mr. R, I hope you like her."

"I'm sure we will. Now you need to get back to your guests and we need to go home to rest. It's an older person thing," I said with a laugh.

Penny said, "Angelo, I haven't seen you this happy since your mother came out to visit. This woman must be special."

"She is. Thanks, Mrs. R. Now I'll go do my job. I'll call you with the date that we'll meet." He stood and smiled, then went off.

"Well, all of our friends are hooked up with a love interest. Glad Angelo has one now. He deserves it," I said.

"I wonder if she knows he was once hooked up with organized crime," Penny said.

"I have a feeling she knows all about him. But I think I may need to look into her past."

"That's terrible. Angelo said he had her checked out. Why do you feel you need to?"

"I don't want to see Angelo hurt. We don't know what this woman could be up to. Angelo said she set up a fake meeting to meet with him. She could be devious."

Network Murders

"Jim, if you ruin this for Angelo, I'll never talk to you again."

"Is that a promise?" I said.

She stared at me then hit my arm. "You are cruel. Now I want to go home and snuggle with Willy in bed. You can sleep on the couch."

I was trying not to laugh. "Okay, shall we go?"

I paid the bill and we said our good-byes to Angelo and went to our car.

As we came into the kitchen, Willy came bouncing out from wherever he was hiding. Penny went to get him his food as I went to my home office. I figured I would get online and do some sneaky checking for Angelo's new girlfriend. I wasn't trying to be mean, but I knew Angelo well enough that if this woman was scamming him, I wanted to stop her. He was tough, but he had a heart. I didn't want to see that break if he got serious for her.

About a half hour later, I heard Penny coming down the hallway so I clicked off the monitor and sat back.

"So did you dig up anything on her?" she asked. "You had enough time to find something."

I smiled. "She seems clean so far. I asked Angelo as we left the restaurant for her full name. Sophia Marie Pascale. She does work for Webster Restaurant Equipment in Henderson. They have a nice website."

Bob Moats

Penny came over and sat on my lap. I didn't protest. She put her arms around me and kissed my cheek. "You are such a good friend. But don't let Angelo know you are checking on her. Unless you find out she's a scumbag."

I gave a look at my wife, amazed at her language. "You have to stop watching those cop shows." I laughed and kissed her back.

Penny stood and said she was going to go to bed and read. "Better be one of my books," I said with a grin.

"No, I don't care for the author," she said then left the room with a laugh.

I clicked the monitor back on and opened up my writing program. I figured that I could get in writing a chapter on my latest book before I hit the sheets.

An hour later I didn't have much written so I shut down the computer. I quietly went to the bedroom. Penny was sitting up on the bed reading. I noticed she had something new on, glasses. In all the time I knew her I never saw her in glasses. She saw me, pulled the glasses off and hid them by her leg.

"Too late, I saw them. I didn't know you wore glasses."

"They're new. I've been having a bit of trouble seeing close up, so I went to an eye doctor last week. It's the price of getting older."

"Not always an old thing. I've worn glasses since I was in fourth grade. I hate them but they are necessary. I

27

can't see without them. I've thought about getting that surgery on my eyes, but it's a little late for me now." I went to the bed and stood, removing my clothes.

"Oh, a strip tease. Yay."

"Don't get excited. I'm tired and going to bed. You can put your glasses back on and read some more."

That's what we did.

The next morning I came out to find Penny at the snack bar reading the newspaper. She had on her glasses and didn't take them off this time. I tried not to laugh.

"You laugh and I'll never talk to you again," she said without looking at me.

"You keep saying that. I'll not laugh just to spare you from not talking to me."

"I may have to revise my statement." She laughed.

I kissed her and we did our morning ritual. She went off to her studio with Willy. She had two days this week to do her show from Vegas before it went national next Monday. I was sure they would have her doing a song and dance about the show.

I finished my morning functions and went to my car. I arrived at my building and went in the back door. Earl was gone, Trapper was out with Sam, and Mac was still at the desk working. Buck wasn't around. I went to the lobby and found a man in a suit standing at the counter, talking to Lacey.

"Jim, this is Mr. Wallace Glass. He's with the CW network and needs help," Lacey said.

The man turned and held out his hand which I took. "Mr. Richards, I need to talk to you."

"Well then, follow me," I said, held the door for him and led him to my office. "Have a seat, please," I said pointing to my client chair. He sat.

"Mr. Glass, are you here about my wife's show?"

"Not that, although I'm hoping it has nothing to do with her show. We are so happy to have her back and this time we are going to be extra careful to keep her. It's about the murder of our west coast head of programming. It happened last night, and I've already talked to the police, but I know you're a bulldog for finding murderers. The police are just too busy to find the killer, which is why I am here," he said.

"I'm sure the police will do the best they can," I said.

"I'm sure they will, but I need you to give your undivided attention to this. The police have too many distractions."

I knew that was true, but I also knew Lynn and Deacon always gave one hundred percent of their attention to a case. I didn't feel the need to explain.

"So you want to hire me to find out what happened?"

"Yes, I'll pay whatever you ask to take care of this before your wife's show goes on. We don't need the distraction of the murder to take away from the premiere. Bad memories from her last show with us. Which is why I don't want just the police to handle this."

*

Chapter 4

"Okay, I'll need all the information you can give me regarding your man," I said.

"His name was Percy Isham. He was in charge of scheduling our shows here on the west coast. It's an important job because shows put in the wrong time slot can ruin the show."

"If there's a wrong time slot, why put a show there?"

"We usually put either a great show or one that we want to phase out. Some shows are just dogs and need to be weeded out to make room for the better shows. The proper time slot can make or break a show. Percy was good at his job. He was working on placing your wife's time slot and the shows that would lead into it. That's important also. A bad show can make people change a channel before a good show can start."

"Did he have the schedule set up, or was he killed before he could finish?"

"Luckily he had the schedule finished before the incident. He emailed his changes to our home office in New York."

"Do you know the name of the detective in charge of the crime scene?" I asked.

"Some woman named Detective Paris," he said.

"Lorelei Paris?" I asked, remembering the female detective who helped during the talent show murders.

"I didn't get her first name. Just Detective Paris."

"Thanks, I'll get in contact with her. We've worked together before. She's as much of a bulldog as I am." I smiled and then said, "Write down all the details I'll need to find you or anyone associated with you in Vegas." I pushed the pad towards him and he started to write. He finished and pushed the pad back.

I looked it over and then said, "I think I have enough for now. If I need more, I'll call you. Thank you and I'll be in touch as soon as I see Detective Paris."

I stood, and then Glass stood. I gave him my business card and led him back to the lobby.

"You can arrange for payment of the retainer with Lacey," I told him and looked at Lacey. She smiled and came to the counter.

"I'll start immediately, Mr. Glass. Thank you for putting your trust in me," I said.

Network Murders

"You did so well back in Michigan when the nut was killing the guests on your wife's show. I trust you."

"Thank you," I said and went back through the door to my office. I wondered how Penny would feel with me getting back in contact with Lorelei. It was business.

I sat at my desk and picked up the phone. After going through my card file I found Lorelei's number and dialed it. She answered after two rings.

"Lorelei, this is Jim Richards. How are you?"

"I'm good, Jim. Good to hear from you. I suspect this call isn't social."

I laughed and said, "No, I've been asked to investigate the murder of Percy Isham. I understand you are the lead in the case."

"I am, and Glass didn't think a woman could solve the case. That's the feeling I got from him. I guess his hiring you proves my point."

"He wants the case solved before my wife's show starts next Monday. He's worried about bad publicity. He feels the police are too distracted to give this the attention it needs."

"He's partially right. We are a bit hard up for officers since there is a case of the flu going around."

"Blue flu? Are the police wanting more money?" I asked.

"No, the real flu. These guys are really sick. One perp comes in with it and it spreads through the jails and to the officers. They should isolate the criminals with sicknesses. I'm trying to hang in. Luckily I had my flu shots."

"Okay, what can you tell me about the case?" I asked.

"As best we can determine, Isham was shot at close range in his office. He was standing at his door when he must have been surprised by an intruder. It was a small caliber gun, probably someone looking to rob the building."

"It was a network office. Would they have anything worth stealing?" I asked.

"I didn't think so. There was no safe, and they didn't handle any cash. Unless Isham knew the perp, I have no idea why he was shot."

"May I see the crime scene?" I asked.

"Sure, you can go in. CSI has finished, and I don't have enough officers to watch the place. The office staff has been told to stay out of the room. If you can find anything, I'd appreciate it. I may end up on traffic duty unless we get a few people well enough to work."

"What if you tell your superiors that you have to meet me at the scene?"

"That might work. When do you think you'll be there?"

"I can go right now. Get you out of the precinct quickly."

"Works for me. Do you know where the building is?"

"Glass gave me the address. I'll find it." We finished and hung up. I went back out to the lobby to tell Lacey I was leaving.

"Is this the network case you're going to check?" she asked.

"Yes, it is. Why?"

"Just making sure you are working. Don't forget to keep track of your records. I expect them turned in on time."

"You are such a task master," I said and went out of the lobby. I could hear her laughing as I walked down the hall to the back door.

In my car, I checked the address and put it in my Android phone's map program. It gave me directions to the building out on South Rainbow Blvd. "Somewhere Over the Rainbow" was stuck in my head, and I kept singing it. I turned the radio on to shake the song from my head and heard a commercial for Penny's show. I turned it up and listened. The network spared no expense to promote her show. They blew it the last time, so they were going to insure they did it right this time.

On the drive I was trying to think of how this murder could be connected to Penny's show. Could this be a copycat of the killer from Michigan during the talk show murders? I had written that book. Could someone have read it and be thinking of repeating the crimes? The killer from before was an employee of the studio. I'd have to take a look at that.

I arrived at the building and parked. I saw a patrol car and hoped Lorelei wasn't going on road duty. I entered the building and went up to a reception desk.

"Hi, I'm here to see the police officer in charge of the murder," I said to the girl.

She smiled, pointed out the door to the hallway and told me where to go. I went there and found Lorelei standing just outside a doorway.

"Jim, you look good. Did you lose some weight?" she asked with a smile.

"No, did you find some weight?" I laughed. "I'm sorry. I haven't lost weight in years so it bothers me when people ask that."

She smiled and apologized. "The crime scene is this way," she said and took me into a large room decorated with posters of TV shows I liked to watch. I wondered if I could get a poster or two.

"This is the outer office. Isham's personal office is there," she said, pointing to a door. There was a dried blood pool on the carpet just inside the door. Must have been where Isham fell after being shot.

Lorelei continued, "He must have been standing in the doorway when he found the intruder. He was shot at close range, so I figure he knew the person. According to his secretary, he was a fixture in the casinos, so this may have been related to his gambling."

"But casinos don't kill their customers. Bookies might. Maybe he had a problem with his gambling debts through them. But that's another problem. Most bookies don't like killing people who owe them money. They can't collect if they're dead. I'll give that some attention, but I don't think it's a lead. This guy was a biggie in the business and must have had money. Was he robbed of his personal effects?"

"CSI found his wallet with plenty of cash, so we don't think it was a robbery. There's no safe in here that we can find. His secretary said there was no cash in the office. We ruled out robbery gone bad," she said.

"So then, this had to be personal. Did his secretary have anything to say about his enemies?"

"I asked. She didn't know of any."

"How about women? Was he having an affair with a married woman? I don't suppose his secretary would know that, but safe to ask," I said.

"I didn't pursue that aspect. May be something good to follow up on."

"I'll chase down that lead. I'm used to tailing spouses." I laughed, thinking about all the cases I had that involved following errant husbands or wives.

"You live a lonely life, don't you?" Lorelei said with a smile.

"Not really. I'm just a peeping tom. I like to watch others fool around," I said, grinning.

"Well, what do you think so far?" she asked.

I walked around the office, studying the room and its contents. I looked around on his desk and saw the sheets for the line-up of the shows. I could see Penny's show listed at eleven in the morning just after a network news/entertainment show, the kind that has five people all sitting around gossiping about celebrities and troubled starlets. That should keep people watching for Penny's show.

"I don't think much yet, but I do think this may be an interesting case."

*

Chapter 5

Lorelei and I left the inner office and I stopped at the secretary's desk. The woman was very attractive and blonde. I guess Isham liked the glamor of sexy looking women around him. I looked at the nameplate on the desk and said, "Miss Clark, may I ask you a couple questions?"

She smiled and said I could.

Network Murders

"How well did you know Isham? I mean his personal life," I asked.

"He was a nice man. He kept to himself. Liked to work late when he was alone," she said.

"Was he alone last night, before he was…well, you know, murdered?"

"As far as I know he was alone. I left at five and he was still in his office. I didn't see him leave."

"Did he get any visitors that might have argued with him or threatened him?" I asked.

"He had a lot of visitors, but they all kissed his ass…pardon me, they were very nice. He was in charge of putting shows on TV, and the people who came to him wanted their shows to be in a good slot. Lots of money was at stake for many of the people who came to him."

"No one wanted him dead, as far as you know?"

"Well, there was one man who came by and I couldn't hear them talking but Mr. Isham seemed very nervous and tense when the man left."

"Do you know who he was?" I asked.

She lifted her appointment book and thumbed through the pages then stopped on one. "Yes, here it is. Joe Callaghan. He didn't say where he was from or what company. I didn't ask. He wasn't nice looking."

I looked at Lorelei and nodded. "Spell that, please," Lorelei requested. The secretary did. She wrote the name in a notepad she took from the pocket of her jacket.

"I'll see what we have on this man," she said to me.

"Callaghan was the only person who might have threatened Isham?" I asked.

"The only one I know. He was a popular person. Everyone liked him."

"Now, on a real personal note, did he have any lady friends?"

"You mean girlfriends? He had a lot of women who enjoyed his company. I never got into his personal life, but they would call here for him. It was easy to see he was involved with them."

"More than one?" I looked at Lorelei and said, "Maybe one was jealous enough to do him in. Two-timing a woman, not healthy." I turned back to the secretary and said, "Know any of these women or where we could find them?"

"Most work at the Golden Slipper. Then there are the women who hang around the casinos."

"You're talking strippers and hookers?" Lorelei asked.

Miss Clark smiled and said yes. "He liked the women who didn't want a commitment, easy to break it off with them."

"Well, it does make sense," I said with a smile. Lorelei just tsked her tongue. "Were any of the women regulars?" I asked.

"There were three of his favorites. They did know of each other and it wasn't a problem for them. As I said, they weren't in it for the commitment. Mr. Isham had lots of money and that's what they were interested in. I personally didn't like it, but that was his business. He wasn't bad looking and could have any woman who wanted a break in TV, but he felt they were using him to further their careers. He liked the women who just wanted to have fun."

"Okay, so no men threatening, and no women feeling used. Not much of a list of suspects. Did Isham have any competition in his job? Someone wanting his position?"

"Listen, everyone in this business wants to get ahead. I wouldn't put it past most of the people in this office to murder to move up the ladder. But everyone here liked Mr. Isham. He was popular."

I turned to Lorelei. "Can I get into his home or apartment, whatever?"

"I was going over there today so you can tag along," she said.

We thanked Miss Clark and left the building. Outside we stood for a moment.

"You still have the red Mustang?" I asked.

"Yep, still have it. You still have the van?"

"Sure do. Penny and I just got back from a two week vacation in it. Up in Washington State," I said.

"Did you get to Seattle?"

"Yep, even climbed the Space Needle. Did you ever get back together with that lawyer?"

"No, he's history. He demanded more than I was willing to give. I'm not giving up police work for him. So I haven't seen him since you and I last worked together. Shall we go?"

"Let's. I'll follow you."

We drove out and up to North Rainbow Boulevard, straight up from Isham's office. There was a condo complex of expensive looking homes. Lorelei pulled up to one building. I parked across from her as there was no parking next to her.

I got out of my car and went to where she stood in front of a door to one condo. She looked back at me and said, "According to my info this is where he lived."

"Do you have a key to get in?" I asked.

"Nope, but I'm prepared," she said taking out a small pouch from her jacket pocket. It had lock pick tools.

"Do you have a search warrant?" I asked.

She turned her head towards me and said with a big smile, "I make my own search warrants."

Network Murders

I was concerned about that, then she said, "Yes, Jim I have a search warrant. I just don't want to wait around for the building super to come and let us in." She managed the door and we went in.

The place was beautiful. Expensive, modern furniture. Large art paintings on the walls that probably cost my entire income for a year. The carpet was thick and soft. I imagined him and one of his ladies rolling around on that in front of the fireplace he had at one end of the room. I didn't understand the fireplace. It was very warm in the room even though the temperature was in the sixties outside.

"So what are we looking for?" Lorelei asked.

"I guess we'll know when we see it. Papers, CDs, email on the computer over on that desk. Someone wanted Isham dead. He may have kept a record of his enemies. Or got a threat."

We heard someone at the door. Lorelei drew her service pistol and I had my hand on my Glock. The door opened and a young man dressed in coveralls with the emblem of the condos on his pocket entered. He saw Lorelei with the gun aimed at him and went pale.

"Hey, I'm not robbing the place," he said quickly. "I saw the patrol car outside and figured you were here. How'd you get in?"

Lorelei smiled and said, "The door was open."

"Strange. I thought it was locked," he replied.

"How would you know it was locked unless you tried the knob?" I asked.

"I heard that the police wanted in so I came by to check the door. I was waiting for someone to show up."

"Well, we're here now. What's your name?"

"Louis Metrone. I'm the super here."

"How well did you know Mr. Isham, Louis?" Lorelei asked.

"He was a cool dude. He liked to party. Are you a cop?" he asked Lorelei.

"Yes, I am, Louis. Now what kind of parties did he have?"

"Well, I probably shouldn't talk bad about the dead, but they were kinky sex parties. Some went on for a couple nights."

"You were around for all the parties?" I asked.

"I have a room on the premises. Sure, I was around. I had to fix the messes his guests made. Damn people would break windows or plumbing. They were crazy people, man. It was easier to be here as the things broke than to come back later. Besides he had great looking women around. I liked to look."

"Did he pay you extra for this service you provided?" I asked.

Network Murders

"Sure he would slip me a couple hundred to keep quiet about his parties. That was dumb. Most of the people in this condo complex knew about his parties."

"And no one called the police?" Lorelei asked.

"Hey, these walls are reinforced with sound proofing about a foot thick. You couldn't hear a gun go off in here. But the other tenants saw the people coming and going, so they figured he had something going on."

"Now tell us if Isham had any fights or people who might have wanted him dead," Lorelei asked.

"Are you kidding? He was a god amongst these people. His funeral will be huge! You can bet on that. There was no person who would hurt him."

"Not one person?" I asked.

He paused and looked like he was thinking. "Well, there was one person who was on Mr. Isham's shit list, Gregg Sando. I think he's part of some mob in Vegas. I happened to hear them arguing one day. Something about drugs. But honestly, Mr. Isham never, ever used drugs. He said it dulled his senses. I liked that."

Lorelei took out her note pad again and wrote in it.

"Louis, who do you think would kill Isham? Your honest opinion," I asked.

He strained again to think. We waited.

"Honestly, I don't know. The women loved him. The men respected him. He was loved by everyone. Sorry, I can't help you on that."

I looked at Lorelei and said, "Now who would want to murder the man everybody loved?"

*

Chapter 6

We thanked Louis and left the condo. Outside we stood looking at the storm clouds forming. Storm Clouds in the Vegas Valley were not something visitors wanted. But it did force them into the casinos where they would spend money. The rain usually poured heavy and then flooded areas of the city. They had storm drains that would take the water away, but not fast enough if it came down hard. I've seen cars floating on the lower land highways and water flooding out of the parking structures behind the Imperial Hotel. The rain would come quickly and leave just as quickly, but there would be a mess after. Then there were the high winds. They came across the valley and I was surprised more of the taller hotel signs didn't topple over.

"I never liked the rain," Lorelei said. "It scares me. I had a bad dream one time that I was floating on a raft out in the middle of a body of water during a storm. No paddle or a way to get to shore. I never felt so frightened."

"One thing about dreams is they aren't real, but when you are in them, it's hard to tell. I'm not fond of dreams either," I said.

"Well, do you need me any more today?" Lorelei asked.

"No, I think I'm all investigated out for today. If I have any questions or problems or answers, I'll call."

"Good. Take care and say hi to Penny."

"I will," I said as she walked to her car. She was still great looking and had fantastic legs. Not that I noticed. Penny was probably reading my mind right about then. I was dead.

I went to the Crown Vic and got in. I sat a moment thinking just as the rains came down, hard. I wasn't going to drive in this mess. A lot of tourists didn't know how to handle the rain. I figured it would stop shortly so I waited.

My cell phone buzzed. It was Lynn. "Hey, mama, what's up?"

"You call me mama one more time and your number will be up," she snarled. "I love my baby girl, but she is driving me crazy. Sleep is not a regular part of our lives now. But we'll survive. Now I called for a reason. I can get Buck in for his P.I. license, just a simple test and paperwork, then you can turn him loose."

"Great, I'll have him call you and set it up. He's starting to bug everyone in the office. Got to get him something to do."

46

"You can give him all the spousal following cases that you don't like."

"True, that will keep him busy. He loves watching people. I'll call him and get this started."

"Don't get wet," she said with a laugh and hung up.

As soon as I hung up the rain passed over me and went off down the valley. The city looked clean and damp now. The valley was under a water drought alert so rain was welcome. I started the car and pulled out of the parking lot. I figured I'd go back to the office to regroup.

I went straight to Buck's office to see if he was bugging Mac. "Is he around?" I asked Mac.

"He was just here, but I think he went to visit with Lacey," Mac said.

That worried me. Lacey probably had Buck in a head lock by now. She doesn't like her routine disturbed and Buck loved to mess with her. I went through the glass doors to find the two of them sitting at Lacey's desk looking friendly. That worried me even more.

"Hey, buddy. What's up?" Buck asked me.

"I got a call from Lynn. She's arranged to get you licensed, so give her a call," I replied.

He shot up from the chair and thanked me. Then he disappeared through the doors to his office.

Network Murders

"Are you going to give him a private office now?" Lacey asked.

"There's room in the storage I can give him," I said with a laugh.

"So what are you up to?" she asked me.

"I have to find a killer. The guy you talked to from the network. I hope this has nothing to do with Penny's show. She wouldn't be very happy if there was murder involved in her premier."

My cell phone buzzed and I took it out. It was Lorelei. I answered, "Hey, just can't get away from me, can you?" Lacey raised one eyebrow when I said that. I went back through the doors to my office to get away from prying ears.

"I got some info on Joe Callaghan," she said.

"That was quick," I replied.

"The wondrous age of computers. Joe Callaghan is a two-bit hood with a connection to a loan shark named Herbert Green. Green has been avoiding prosecution through a bunch of shyster lawyers."

I laughed thinking about my favorite shyster lawyer, Alphonse Grisler, now serving time for his murderous attempts.

"Callaghan has nothing on his rap sheet about murdering anyone. Mostly minor felony charges for petty crimes. Then I checked on Gregg Sando, and he has been a really bad boy. Again the shyster lawyers kept him from prison on charges of attempted murder a couple of times. The lawyers got him off on technicalities in his arrests. Now I'm glad I broke up with my lawyer boyfriend."

"Yes, you deserve better. So do you know where Sando hangs out?"

"He's part of a bunch of gang bangers who have a club on the south of town. The Shady Lady, it's called. Not a nice place to go if you're thinking of it."

"I have a partner or two who could help me there. One is an ex-biker and he's nothing to be trifled with. The other is an ex-CIA spook who loves to bash heads. So I'm covered if I do go there."

"I hope so. I can't help much. They have me on double duty until we get men back from sickness. Call if you need help. Oh, and how are Lynn and Deacon doing?"

"They're a bit frazzled from sleepless nights. The baby has been keeping them up."

"Good reason for me not to have children. I like my sleep. Well, as I said, call if you need me."

"I will, take care," I said and hung up.

I sat back in my chair when I heard the doors to the lobby open and close. I was expecting Lacey but it was someone better. Penny. She was carrying Willy and set him down on the floor as she entered.

"Hi, sweetie. Catch any dangerous killers today?"

Network Murders

"I'm working on it. Sit down. I have something to tell you."

She gave me a quizzical look and sat. I felt a tug at my cuff and reached down to pick up Willy. I sat him on my desk as he tried to jump on me.

"So what's up? Should I worry?" she asked.

"I don't think so, but you may hear about it. I'd rather be the one to tell you."

"Is this about the murder of the network guy?" she said.

That took me by surprise. "How did you know?"

"I hear lots of things that involve the station and the network now. Gordy sat me down to talk about it. He said he doubted it had anything to do with my show next week. I agreed after he explained."

"Good to see Gordy is on top of the news," I said.

"Jim, he's a producer at the station, he hears everything that goes on there. The morning news even mentioned it. Gordy thinks it may help my following if everyone thinks this is connected to my show. I'm not happy about it, but if it will bring in more viewers, fine."

"You are a cold woman. Using some guy's death to further your career."

"Hey, he's dead. Not much I can do about that. It's your job now to find the killer."

"How did you know I was investigating the murder?" I asked.

"A little bird told me," she said with a smile.

"A little buzzard named Lacey I'll bet."

"Hey, she's not a buzzard. She's a songbird."

"Yeah, well, she sings too much. So what are you up to yourself?"

"I thought we'd go to lunch. I'm starving."

"It will have to be fast food. I have to go question a bad guy. How's Sonic sound?"

"Sounds fattening, but I could go for it. Although all that fancy food Carol's been making at Angelo's restaurant is just as fattening."

I stood and took Willy off the desk where he had plopped down to nap. He gave me a look and I tucked him in my arm. We went out to the lobby and told Lacey we were leaving. I gave Willy to Lacey and she put him on her desk. He plopped down again.

I asked Penny, "Is Willy getting enough sleep or is he vitamin deficient?"

"He's just getting lazy, like someone I know."

"Hey, you better not mean me," I said as I followed her out the front door to her car. We said our hellos to Tracey in the outer lobby and left the building.

"You can drive, I'm relaxing," I said.

"And you wonder why Willy is getting lazy."

We drove to a nearby Sonic and parked. We ordered through the box and relaxed until our food came out to our car by a waitress on roller skates.

"I was too young to appreciate car-hops at drive-in restaurants in the fifties. It's nice this place still holds to that tradition."

"Sure, you like anything that keeps you from having to getting out of the car to eat," Penny said as she took a big bite of her burger.

*

Chapter 7

We finished our lunch and were waiting for the car-hop to get the tray when my cell phone buzzed. I looked at the caller ID and it was Lorelei again. I debated answering it since I was with Penny, but this was a job, not pleasure.

"Hello," I said.

"Jim, it's me again. I just wanted to tell you that Joe Callaghan has been in lockup for the last two days awaiting trial. He couldn't have murdered Isham. Are you going to still talk to Sando?"

"I'm at lunch right now with Penny, but when I get back to the office, I'll see who's available to go with me."

"Say hi to Penny for me and be careful at the bar," she said.

"I will, thanks," I said and hung up.

"One of your girlfriends?" Penny asked.

"Yes, if you must know, Lorelei Paris. She's the lead detective on the network guy murder," I said carefully.

"And you were going to tell me this when?" she said with a sly smile.

I thought, never, I had hoped. "It was going to come up eventually."

"Is she still a fox?" Penny was enjoying this interrogation.

"What do you think? She got ugly? Of course she's good looking. But I don't look, it's strictly business."

"Bull rippy. Just don't touch."

"I doubt I'll see her again, she's busy," I said wanting to change the subject. Penny loved to harass me when she could.

"Doesn't matter, she's in your head now. That's as far as you can go." She started the car as soon as the girl took the tray. We headed back to the office and into the building.

Network Murders

Willy was running around the lobby and came to us. Penny picked him up.

Lacey stood and walked to the counter. She pointed to a woman sitting in our waiting area. I turned and saw a very good looking woman, quite sexy even. I felt Penny gently hit my arm. I gave her a nasty look and went to the woman.

"Hi, I'm Jim Richards. May I help you?" I put on my best smile for the woman.

"Mr. Richards, I heard you are investigating the murder of Percy?" she said, smiling with a mouth full of big straight teeth. They looked too big for her mouth, making me wonder if they were real. I didn't ask.

"If you are referring to Percy Isham, I am investigating, yes. Did you know the deceased?"

"I was a close personal friend of his," she said.

I could imagine how close. "What can I do for you?"

"May we talk in private?" she said, eyeing Penny and Lacey.

"Of course, please follow me." I held her hand to help her up. She had on a tight short skirt that almost exposed her panties as she rose. I didn't look. Mostly because Penny was watching.

I took her to the doors for the offices and opened them for her. She went in, and I looked back to see the two women eyeing me. I stuck my tongue out and went in quickly before Penny could throw something. I led the woman to my office and had her sit. I went around my desk and sat also.

"Now, Miss, what is it you want?" I asked again.

"I'm Molly Sharp, I hope I can help you with this crime. I know who may have killed Percy," she said quietly as though someone might hear.

"That would be very nice, Molly," I replied quietly back. "Who do you think did it?"

"It was a cop," she said.

I waited, then when she said nothing else, asked, "Okay, why a cop?"

"Percy said he had a cop after his ass. Something about money he owed a bookie," she replied.

"Why would a cop help a bookie collect?" I asked.

"I don't know, but Percy wasn't happy. He felt all the cops were ganging up on him."

"Did Percy have mental problems?"

She stared at me for a moment. "Not that I knew. He was always normal around me. What kind of mental problems do you mean?"

"Oh, paranoia or fear of police. Did he talk to himself at all?"

"Not that I remember. He was a kind man. Very sensitive and caring. I worried for him when he told me that there was a cop bothering him."

"Okay, do you know the cop's name?" I asked.

"He only mentioned a first name, Nate. Yes, it was Nate."

"It's an unusual name. I should be able to track him down. I want to thank you for coming forward with this. Just who was it who told you I was on the case?"

"I heard from Wallace, Percy's boss."

"Wallace Glass?"

"Yes, Wally. He's another nice man." She smiled.

I was getting the idea that Wally and Percy shared women. Maybe he liked to participate at Percy's sex orgies.

"So is this Nate the only person you know who may have wanted to have Percy hurt?"

"That's all I know. I just wanted to share this to help your case," she said with a smile that would melt butter. I had to keep focused.

I stood and came around my desk to her. "Thank you so much. I'll do some checking on this Nate person and see if it helps."

She stood and went to the door. I followed her out to the front where Penny and Lacey were still standing from when I left them. I knew there would be an inquisition.

"Thank you again for your information. It will help me investigate," I said, and she went out the front door. I didn't watch her. I turned my attention to Penny. She was smirking.

"Have a nice visit with the peroxide playmate?" Penny asked.

"I'm sure her hair is natural. And she was helpful, giving me new info into the death of the network man," I replied.

"Do you think it has anything to do with my show coming back?" Penny asked.

"No, I don't. It's looking like this guy was a player and may have crossed lines somewhere. Either gambling or with women, but he did something wrong. I can't see a connection to your show so far."

"I hope not. I don't want to start this new show with murders. I had enough of that back in Michigan," Penny said, scrunching up her face.

"Well, we'll be prepared for whoever this time," I said.

The front door opened and Buck came in. "Break out the bubbly. I'm now an official P.I. for the firm!" he said with a cheer.

Network Murders

"Congratulations, Buck!" I said. "That was quick. Did Lynn push it through?"

"She did. Pulled some strings. I have to wait for my license to come from Nevada's State Attorney General, but Lynn said I could work under your license still. She gave me a cute little temporary card."

"Good, now you can help me with this new case I just got. I need to go talk to a hood at a bar he hangs at. You are just what I need."

"I'm ready, willing and able now." He gave me his famous walrus smile. "When do we go?"

"Right now, if you are ready."

"Let's roll. I'll drive." He smiled at Penny and Lacey and said, "This is a momentous day, remember it well."

The women cheered him on as he turned to the door followed by me. I looked back and said, "I'm glad his head fits through the door."

We went to Buck's T-Bird and I got in the passenger seat. He started the car up and revved it a couple times. Like a lion roaring, I thought. I was happy for Buck. He worked so hard to get the security company going, and now it was good to have him back helping me.

"Where to?" he asked.

I gave him the directions to the Shady Lady.

"Hey, is this a strip club?" he asked.

"Honestly, I don't know. It could be. I've never been there before. I guess we'll find out."

He pulled out of the parking lot and drove off. About ten minutes later we arrived and found that it was a strip club. That made Buck happy. He parked and we went in. It was dark except for the lights of the stage where a very tired looking woman was attempting to dance. The back bar was lit, providing the only other light in the room. I wondered if Sando would be here. There were about five rough looking men sitting at a table in the back giving us the eye.

I wasn't worried with Buck along.

*

Chapter 8

We sat at a table near the stage and then a much too young looking waitress came up. I was thinking of asking her how old she was when Buck spoke.

"Just how old are you, little girl?" he said with his smooth voice.

She didn't say anything at first, then, "I'm eighteen, just young looking. Why? Are you the cops?"

Network Murders

"Nope, just wondering. I hope you stay young looking the rest of your life. Just get away from this place if you want to live a long and healthy lifetime," Buck said.

"It's a job, not easy to find in this town. Now what would you like to drink?" she asked.

Buck said, "Diet Sprite if you have it." She said they did then looked at me.

Buck was driving, so I said, "A draft, please."

She went off as we turned our attentions to the stage, now occupied by a much better looking dancer than the last. Our drinks came back and I asked, "Is Sando in?"

She gave me a frown and said, "You don't know him?"

"No, that's why I'm asking."

"He's sitting with his crew at the back table. You don't want to mess with them."

I smiled, thanked her, paid for the drinks and gave her a big tip. She smiled and went off. Buck and I watched the new girl dancing until she finished and a new dancer came up.

"Shall we go talk to Sando now?" Buck asked

"No, I'd like to finish my drink first. Then we'll go talk nice with the crew."

Bob Moats

Buck smiled and took another sip of his Sprite. I was watching the men at the back of the room. There were four sitting at the table with one sitting just outside the circle. I assumed he was Sando, he looked arrogant enough. His men looked like rejects from a carnival. I wasn't worried. With Buck there I felt safe. He was huge, had muscles stretching his t-shirt and was a former biker. He didn't let anyone mess with him. Although he was sensitive, he could be dangerous.

We watched the new dancer until she finished, then I looked at Buck and said, "I'm ready."

He downed what was left of his drink and then stood, all six foot three of him. We walked to the men, Buck on my left.

I went to the man sitting away from the table and said, "Excuse me, are you Gregg Sando?"

He looked up at me and said, "You aren't the cops, just a nosey person looking to get hurt."

I noticed his men were straightening up and moving their hands to their sides. Buck brought his .38 up and pushed it into Sando's head.

"You men may need to relax and put your hands on the table, empty. Or I'll ventilate your boss' brain. I don't care one way or the other, but it's up to Mr. Sando," Buck said loudly with his tough voice. I was trying not to smile as I pulled my jacket back to show my Glock.

Network Murders

Sando finally spoke. "Relax, I'll handle this." His men did relax a bit but were still on alert. "What do you want?" he asked.

"Can you follow us?" I said as Buck pushed his gun harder into Sando's head.

"Okay, don't get trigger happy, Hulk." Sando stood and I led him back to our table. Buck was watching the men, still waiting for something to happen.

I had Sando sit with his back to his men so he couldn't signal them and to put him between us and his crew in case they tried to shoot us.

Sando looked uncomfortable with this position. "I'm sorry, but I'm not taking any chances. So just sit there and talk to us. We don't bite," I said.

Buck smiled and said, "But I do shoot."

"I get it. Are you from another mob?" he asked.

"Oh, hell no. We are on the side of truth, justice and the American way. I'm a private investigator hired to find out what happened to Percy Isham. This is my associate, he busts heads."

Buck laughed out loud but kept his gun trained on Sando.

I leaned forward to him and said, "I'm not wanting to hurt you, but I'd like to know what your business was with Isham."

"You're not a cop?" he said to cover his ass.

"Nope, and this is not a sting. I just want to get to the bottom of the murder."

He sat staring for a long while then said, "I had dealings with him to provide some fun ingredients for his orgies. He wanted more, and my friends didn't want to keep providing him without payment. I shouldn't have given him any without money. My bad."

"So you threatened him to get him to pay up?"

"I may have tried to convince him to do so. But I wouldn't kill him. That would be stupid to lose the money he owed."

The same logic I told Lorelei. "So now that he's dead, what are you going to do?"

"I'm not going to lose out. He had a stash of cash that I am going to find. Then I'll be able to pay back his debt and have a little left for myself."

"How did you know about his stash?" I asked.

"He talked too much in bed. One of his girls works for my contacts. She mentioned his bragging."

"I don't suppose you know where the money is."

"Not yet, but I will. Besides, I wouldn't tell you if I did."

Network Murders

Buck smiled and said, "You aren't a very nice person, Sando. Watch your back one dark lonely night."

"Is that a threat?" Sando asked.

"No, it's a promise," Buck said quietly through his teeth.

I stood watching the idiots at the back of the room. "I'm done with you, Sando. Now that didn't hurt, did it?"

Sando didn't say anything as Buck stood, putting his gun back in its holster. He aimed with his finger at Sando and went, "Bang."

We left the bar still watching our backs. Sando didn't move from his chair. The men stood and came forward to him. We were out in the sunshine again and went to Buck's car.

"Did we learn anything?" Buck asked.

"Honestly, I'm not sure. We know now that Isham was into drugs for his guests at his parties. But I was told he didn't indulge in them himself. I'll have to ask Joe Lang after he autopsies the body if he had drugs in his system."

"It's nice to have people in the right positions," Buck said.

I smiled and said, "Yes, it is. Makes my life easier. Now having you around will also help. I never would have survived going into that bar by myself."

"You always have your Glock," he said.

"Yes, but I'm getting to the point where it's getting harder to move fast."

"You aren't saying that you are getting old are you?" he said, sounding amazed.

"I think I'm getting arthritis in my arms. It worries me, but I'll survive."

"I'll need to take you out to a gym to work it out."

"This sort of thing doesn't just work out with exercise, Buck. It's a condition that doesn't go away easily. There are medicines to make the pain go away. But I hate using drugs, even if they help."

"Well, if they help, I'll make sure you take your medicine," he said with a grin.

"Thank you, Buck, you are a true friend. Now shall we go back to the office? I have no more places to go right now."

He drove over to our building and pulled in the back. We went through the back door, setting off Lacey's alarm. I waved to the camera. Buck said he was going to check on Mac, and I went to the front. Penny was not around, and for that matter neither was Lacey. I was surprised to see Tracey at Lacey's desk.

"Tracey, where are Lacey and my wife?" I asked.

Tracey blushed and said, "They went shopping."

"That's something Penny had to organize. Did they say what the occasion was for a shopping spree?"

"Penny's show premier. She wants everyone here to attend the taping. I'm invited too," she said, sounding happy.

"That's nice, but I thought Penny had all the clothes she needs from our trip to Washington State."

"Oh, it's not for Penny, it's for Lacey. She was saying she had nothing nice to wear, so Penny kidnapped her to get some clothes."

I could imagine how many items of clothing Penny would buy. Now that she was going to make more money for her show, clothes were no longer a luxury.

"I'm happy for the both of them. As long as Penny doesn't go broke."

"No, she said she was going to use your charge card," Tracey said, then realized what she said. "Oops, I wasn't supposed to tell you that."

"Don't worry. I'll keep your secret safe. Until the bill comes in." I turned and went to my office. Willy was sleeping on my desk. I picked him up, and he groggily came around. I put him on the client chair and sat at my desk.

I went through my card index to find Joe Lang's private number. I dialed and waited for him to answer. He came on after six rings. I thought he might not answer if he had his hands in some dead person's open chest. That image made my stomach turn.

"Jim, what can I do for you?" he asked.

"I just wanted to find out what you found on Percy Isham's body."

He said, "Got a while to talk?"

*

Chapter 9

"I'm all ears," I said as I sat back in my chair. "Whatcha got?"

"Isham was murdered," Joe said with a subdued laugh.

"That much we already know. Got something more interesting?"

"Single gunshot to the head. Good clean shot, 9mm."

"Police use 9mm, don't they?" I said, thinking about what the bleached blonde Molly told me about the cop.

"Usually, but so do criminals. I sent the bullet to be checked. Maybe we'll get lucky if it is a cop. All weapons used by our police have had their gun barrels registered."

Network Murders

"Any drugs found in his system?" I asked.

"The guy was clean for drugs other than his liver was ready to explode. He was a heavy drinker. He had a high level of alcohol in his system when he was killed. He must have been drinking in the office. Oh, and he had AIDS."

That gave me a chill. "Gee, when were you going to bring that up?" I said with a smile. "Was it bad enough to spread to other sexual partners?"

"Yep, could be a reason for murdering him. Maybe he gave it to someone and they didn't like it."

I said, "He had sex parties often at his house. I wonder how many people he gave it to."

"That's one thing an autopsy can't tell. You'll have to talk to anyone who may have attended his parties. Get to them to be checked before they spread it to others. I'm calling Lorelei on this now. It's her case."

"I was hired by Isham's boss to find the killer, so it's sort of my case too."

"I can't say if Isham knew about the AIDS, but he was not going to live forever. It was just a matter of time before he would be dead from it. The killer may have done him a favor."

"Call Lorelei and tell her. I'll call her in a while to see what she wants to do. Thanks, Joe."

"My pleasure. How are Deacon and Lynn doing with the baby?"

"Good as far as I know. I need to visit them before they think I don't care. Thanks again," I said and hung up.

I sat back further in my chair thinking about what Joe had told me. You don't hear much about AIDs anymore, although it's still out there. The media has gone on to other things, like the economy or how bad the president is doing. Yeah, important things like that. I need to get hold of Molly Sharp and find out how far she went with Isham. Then talk to Louis Metrone, the super at Isham's condo. Get a fix on how far the sex orgies went.

"Are we investigating anymore today?" came a voice from my doorway. It was Buck. I almost fell over in my chair when he spoke. I straightened up.

"I just found some more information that will make a lot of people unhappy. Isham had AIDS," I said.

"Are you serious?" he asked.

"Like death. We need to go visit another strip club. I'm sure you'll enjoy that."

"Hell yeah. Which club?"

"Golden Slipper, up on the Boulevard above Charleston. Shall we go?"

"Aye, Captain, full sails ahead," Buck said.

I stood, picking up Willy, and just stared at him. "Are you getting into sailing now?"

"No, that's from Star Trek," he said with a smile.

Network Murders

"I think you mean full speed ahead. Warp drives on full," I said trying to remember the technical terms.

He smiled and followed me to the front lobby. "Tracey, tell Penny, if she returns alive, that I'll see her at home."

"Will do, boss," she said as I handed her Willy. She took the dog and set him on the desk.

Buck and I went to my car this time and drove out to the strip. Traffic was light and we made good time heading up the boulevard. We arrived at the club in good time. I hoped that Molly was working. Or at least any other dancer who might have attended Isham's parties. I parked and we went in. I had been there before so knew the lay of the land. I laughed, thinking on that statement. There were three dancers entertaining on three stages. Lights were flashing and pulsating around the room. We went to a table near the middle stage and sat.

A waitress came up and I asked, "Is Molly working today?"

"Which Molly?" she asked.

"Molly Sharp," I replied.

"Yeah, Candy Cane, she's up shortly. Now what do you want to drink?"

We ordered and she went off. Buck and I watched the dancers until our drinks came. I paid and the girl went off again. About ten minutes later Molly or Candy Cane came out and up to the middle stage. She started to dance then she saw me and did a double take. She caught herself and continued to dance. But she had her eye on me.

She did her three dances on stage and came down to us. "Well, Mr. P.I., what are you doing here?"

"We need to talk," I said.

"I can't just talk, but I could give you a lap dance and then we can talk."

I took out a twenty and told her to give Buck a lap dance, but face me. Buck's eyes went big and nearly rolled up in his head. I smiled.

Molly sat on Buck's lap, and I said, "I need to tell you something important. First though, did you have sex with Isham?"

"Oh, heaven's no. He didn't like women. He was gay or I should say, bi," she said.

That really threw me. "Do you know any of the men he may have…" I didn't want to say it.

"Screwed? Is that what you are trying to say?" she said moving around on Buck. He was loving the ride.

"Yeah, I guess that's what I wanted to say. Do you know?"

"There was a couple men he spent time with. Wally was one."

Network Murders

That also threw me. "Wallace Glass? The network guy?"

"Yep, that's him, Percy's boss. He was bi and so were most of the men there. I'm bi also. I like men and women. But Percy was mostly gay. He liked men, but I heard he had women occasionally. He usually had women around to have on his arm in public, to give the appearance of being straight."

The dance ended and Molly got up. Buck was grinning from ear to ear. "Molly, I have to tell you something and it's important. Did you have sex with any of the men who had sex with Percy?"

"I suppose so. We all went around with each other," she replied.

"You need to go to a doctor and get checked for AIDS. Isham had it and it could be spread to you," I said, trying to be subtle.

Her eyes got big and she made a face that told me she was ready to have a fit. "Are you saying Percy had AIDS? And I could have it?" she said loudly.

"I don't know if you have it. You need to be checked, and fast."

She left us and went off to the back room. I figured that we had done enough damage here. "Shall we get out of here and go see the network boss?"

"I don't know if I can stand," he said, looking down at his crotch.

"Shall I pour cold water on it?" I said with a grin.

"No, I'll keep it for a while." He stood carefully and we went out of the club.

Back in the car he said, "Damn, it's gone. Oh well."

"You'll live. Now I need to talk to Glass to see if he knows he may have AIDS."

Buck exhaled and said, "Thank goodness I don't have random sex. Maria and I enjoy our sex life, as sparse as it is."

"Not getting much?" I asked, not really wanting to know. Maria was Deacon's sister and the thought of her having sex with Buck must be hard enough on Deacon.

"We've cooled off, so we just enjoy each other's company. Maria isn't a sexual person. Funny, since she dances topless in the Tropicana show. I guess she gets enough of flashing her boobs for the audiences and the drooling men."

"I can see if you do something too often it gets old." I had pulled out of the club and was heading to the network offices again.

On the way my cell phone buzzed. I pulled into a parking lot for a drug store and looked at the caller ID. It was Lorelei.

"Hey, girl, did you talk to Joe Lang?" I put it on speaker so Buck could hear.

"I did. And this is going in a new direction. What are you up to?"

"I talked to a stripper who attended Isham's parties. She told me something interesting. Isham was gay."

"Are you serious?" she asked.

"Why is everyone asking me that? I wouldn't say it if it wasn't true."

"So we are getting conflicting stories. The super said he had sex parties."

"But he didn't say who was having sex with who. Buck and I are heading to see Wallace Glass. My source says he was involved in the sex parties."

"Buck? Is that your security boss?"

"He is. He's now licensed to investigate. We just left the strip bar and are going to see Glass."

"Strip bar. Boy, you are having fun, aren't you?"

"Not really. Buck got the lap dance. I just asked questions."

"Poor baby, but I'm sure Penny would appreciate your restraint," she said. "Are you going to tell her?"

"Are you crazy? Besides, she probably already knows. I'm dead as of this afternoon. Remember, she'll be the main suspect in my murder."

Chapter 10

"Are you going to talk to Glass now?" she asked.

"That's the plan. I don't know if he knew about the AIDS. If so, he might have a motive for murder."

"I'd join you but I'm pulling desk duty until this flu epidemic ends. I'm thinking of calling in sick tomorrow myself. Let me know what you find. I'd appreciate the help."

I smiled and said, "I'll solve the case for you, just don't get sick."

We said our good-byes and hung up. Buck asked about the flu.

"It's not a blue flu. They aren't going for more money or better hours. They are supposedly really sick. It's like my son says, he takes my grandson to school and the kid comes back with all kinds of illnesses."

"I haven't been sick in years. I never liked being ill," Buck said.

"Neither did I. Here we are," I said as I pulled into the drive to the network offices that Isham had set up for them. I parked and we went in.

Network Murders

The place hadn't changed. There was no mourning for Isham, just a busy day for the workers. We went to the same secretary that Lorelei and I had talked to earlier.

She smiled and asked, "Would you like to see Mr. Anderson?"

I was confused. "Who's Mr. Anderson?"

"He took over for Mr. Isham," she replied matter of factly.

I looked at Buck and said, "The body hasn't even gone into rigor yet and they go on." I looked back at the secretary. "Is he busy?"

"Hold on, I'll see." She lifted the phone and called in. She explained the situation then hung up. "He's on a call from the network in New York. He'll be with you shortly," she said with a smile.

Buck and I wandered around the room looking at posters of TV shows running on the network. I came to one about Penny's new show. It was placed where it could be seen easily by anyone coming into the office. They had a nice photo of Penny, but it was from the last time she was doing her show from Detroit. At least they could have updated the thing. She still looked good. I hoped she had a good response as she did from her prior show. Judging from everyone who recognized her on the road, she should do well. If the network played their cards right and gave her new show the publicity it needed.

Buck finally plopped down on a couch and huffed. I was getting tired of waiting also and went to the girl at the desk.

"Is Anderson still busy?" I asked.

She looked at her phone and saw the light still on. "Yes, he's still on the phone. Sorry."

"Fine, can you direct me to Wallace Glass' office?" I was getting impatient.

"Do you have an appointment with Mr. Glass?" she asked politely.

Right then I wanted to strangle someone and she was close. "Mr. Glass hired me to find the killer of Isham. I think he would want to talk to me. Now direct me to his office or I'll start yelling his name out until he answers."

She paled slightly and stood, taking me to the door to the hallway. Buck got up and followed us out. She pointed down the hallway and said, "His office is there. The secretary should be able to help you."

I gave her my biggest smile and said, "Thank you, you have been very helpful. Oh, and tell Anderson he is rude."

Buck and I left her standing with her mouth open and went to the new office. We entered and there was another attractive female at the desk. I wondered if any woman over 40 worked there.

She smiled and asked if she could help us.

Network Murders

"Yes, tell Glass that Jim Richards is here to see him. Very important business about Percy Isham."

She lost her smile and picked up the phone. She spoke briefly and then hung up.

"You can go right in," she said.

I heard Buck mutter, "That's better."

I opened the door and we went in. This office was a bit gaudier than the former Isham's office. It had all kinds of award plaques, photos of stars and the usual posters. It had potted plants all around the room making it look like a rain forest.

Glass was sitting behind an oversized desk that looked like an expensively made teakwood desk. All carved and ornate in decorations. He stood as we approached and held out his hand.

I shook it and introduced Buck.

"Mr. Glass, this is my associate, Buck Carson. He's the brawn of our team," I said.

"Good to meet you, Mr. Carson. Please sit, both of you. Do you have anything to tell me about Percy?"

"Well, it's going to depend on you. I'm still hunting leads about who killed him. But in my investigations I came across some information that I'm sure will affect you and others."

He got a serious look on his face. "And what would that be?" he asked.

I paused, not really wanting to give him a possible death sentence. I cleared my throat and finally said, "Did you know that Isham had AIDS?"

Glass suddenly went pale, whiter than his shirt. He sat back in his chair and looked like he was going to have a coronary. I was just going to ask if he was all right when he spoke.

"Are you totally sure of your statement?"

"I talked to the medical examiner that performed the autopsy. I'm sure he wasn't happy to find the victim had AIDS. So I'd say it's a sure thing."

Glass put his head back and stared at the far wall.

"Mr. Glass, I've talked to a young lady named Molly Sharp. Do you know her?"

He looked puzzled.

"She also goes by Candy Cane. Does that ring a bell?" I asked.

Now I could see recognition in his eyes. "Yes, I do know Miss Cane." He paused then said, "Oh, God, does she have AIDS also?"

"I think she's getting checked shortly so I can't say, but she tells me an interesting tale. Seems you and Isham were very close." I waited for his response.

Network Murders

He didn't say anything at first, then he asked, "Is what I tell you confidential?"

"Other than the law asking me, I won't tell a soul," I replied.

"Then, coming from Candy, you already know about Percy and me. Yes, we were partners in a sense. I'm not ready to be involved with anyone on a permanent basis and since Percy was bi-sexual, mostly for men, I wasn't involved closely with him other than his parties." He reached to a pitcher on his desk and poured a glass of water. He drank it all down and set the glass on the desk.

"What do I need to know about the parties? I mean, anyone there who had relations with Isham could have contracted AIDS. It would be a motive for murder if Isham hadn't told others about his condition."

Glass looked at me like I was accusing him of murder. "I would never kill Percy. Even if I had found out about the AIDS. I certainly hope you aren't insinuating that."

"No, I'm not accusing anyone at this point, but I need to know who all may have been involved sexually with him. Can you help with that?"

"Talk to Candy. She knows most of the people who attend the parties. Or you could talk to that little creep of a super at the condos. I think his name is Lonnie."

"Louis," I corrected.

"Yeah, Louis. He was always skulking around watching everyone. He's a piece of work. As for me, I need to go see a doctor, quickly. So if you have nothing further, I'll ask you to leave." He stood and headed for the door.

Buck and I stood. "I'd say he didn't know about the AIDS," Buck said.

"Nope. I think I've had enough of this for today. Too many people have been given bad news. I'd like to hear some good news. Shall we go back to the office and battle with Lacey and Penny over their purchases?"

"I'd say that's a winner," Buck said with a smile.

We left the building and went back to the car. Arriving back at the office we went in the front door. The outer lobby was empty with a sign saying to go into the building. So we went into the main lobby where we found what amounted to a fashion show.

*

Chapter 11

Buck and I stood at the door watching Penny and Lacey holding up the various dresses and clothing from a number of packages spread around the lobby. Penny suddenly saw us and smiled.

"Hey, sweetie, come see what Lacey and I bought for her," she said.

Network Murders

I said to Buck, quietly, "With my charge card." I stepped over the packages to Penny and stood next to her. She held up a skirt to me and I backed away. "No, thank you, I'm not ready to change clothes."

Penny laughed and kissed me. "No matter what kind of clothes you wear, I still love you."

"So did you blow my entire budget for the month?" I asked.

"Not quite, but I can go out and finish it off if you insist." She gave me her devilish grin.

"Please leave me a little for some burgers and fries. Now that you've outfitted Lacey, have you decided what you're going to wear?"

"Of course. I'd still be home if I hadn't figured on the perfect outfit yet."

I looked at an opened dress box on the counter and saw Willy inside fighting with the fancy tissue that said it had contained an expensive article of clothing. He had just about wrapped himself up in the paper as I reached over to extricate him before he smothered. He licked my hand as I held him.

"So have you caught your killer yet?" Penny asked.

"Still working on it. You'll be relieved to know that I don't think the killing had anything to do with your show," I replied.

"Good, I don't want anything to mar my premiere. How's foxy lady doing?"

"I wouldn't know other than she's busy at work. I talked to her on the phone briefly this morning, and she's doing double duty since half the police force is out with illness."

"Lots of flu going around, I hear. Don't you catch it while you're out gallivanting around the city. I'm not going on my first show throwing up in a bucket on the stage."

"I'll get you one of those surgical masks to wear until then." I kissed her on the lips gently and signaled to Buck. We left the lobby, going to my office. "You live an amazing life, Jim," Buck said with a laugh.

"I'll give it to you if you'll take the expenses. I have the money but after Penny finishes with me, I'll be down on the south strip sleeping in a doorway."

We entered my office. I put Willy on the desk and sat. I picked up the phone and dialed Lorelei, then she came on after a couple rings. I told her it was me and put her on speaker.

"So what did you come up with?" she asked.

"Glass wasn't aware that Isham had AIDS. He got real upset when we told him. I asked if he knew anyone else who attended the parties, but he told me to go talk to the stripper and, surprisingly, Louis. Glass has a low opinion of Louis."

"After talking to Louis, I have a low opinion of him, too. What are you going to do now?"

"I'm taking the rest of the day off. I haven't visited with Lynn and Deacon to see the baby much. So that's my agenda for the rest of the day."

"Well, say hi for me and tell them I'm thinking of them," she said.

"I will and if I hear anything more, I'll call."

We finished and hung up. I sat back and looked at Buck. He was scratching Willy behind the ears. Willy was loving it.

"So, I'm finished with investigating. What are you going to do now?" I asked Buck.

"I think I'll take Maria out for a nice dinner to celebrate my becoming a P.I. and then maybe we'll take a ride around the city on my Harley."

"Just watch out for the tourists on the roads. I need you back safe and sound." I stood and picked up Willy. Buck followed me out and back to the lobby. I was amazed that the women had all the packages re-boxed and back in bags, ready to go.

"Did you decide on what Lacey's going to wear to the premiere?" I asked Penny.

"Yep, all picked out and ready to go. What are we up to?" she asked.

"I haven't spent much time with Lynn and Deacon, so we will go see the baby. If you can fit it in your schedule."

"That's good with me. I'll help Lacey put these things in her car and we can go home to freshen up." She went to get packages with Lacey who was giving me a big smile. They carried as much as they could handle to the back parking lot to Lacey's car.

Buck said, "I should go see if the security guards haven't tied up Mac yet." He turned and went to his office. I stood looking at Tracey sitting by herself at Lacey's desk.

"Do you have an outfit to wear for the show?" I asked.

"Are you kidding? I love clothes and have way too many to choose from. I'm good," she replied.

"I guess everyone is ready then." Penny came back in and up to me.

"Lacey is going to get the rest of her stuff. We can go. I'll follow you home." She turned and went out to her car as I went out to mine.

Follow wasn't the operative term. She beat me back to the house and was already in. I walked into the kitchen as she was feeding Willy and said I was going to take a quick shower.

"Care to join me?" I asked.

Network Murders

"Don't start that. Go clean up and we'll go. I'll call Lynn to be sure they are ready for guests."

"True, we might have gone there and found them sitting around in their underwear. Not a pretty sight," I said.

"Will you stop that and go get ready?" Penny pushed me out of the kitchen and went to the phone.

Forty minutes later, we were ready to go. I pulled the Crown Vic out of the garage as Penny locked Willy in the kitchen. He was getting used to it. Penny said as she got into the car that they were happy to have us over.

"I hope so. I haven't been there more than twice since they had the baby," I said.

"Well, if you'd stop playing detective once in a while you'd have more time to visit."

"Our two week vacation didn't help either. The baby is probably walking by now," I said.

"I doubt that. Please don't talk about crime while we visit. Let's just have a nice evening with our friends," she said.

"Believe me, I'm sure the conversation will be about little Penny tonight." I said.

"Little Penny," she laughed. "I feel sorry for the child."

I finally pulled into the drive of their apartment building and parked. We went to the front door as it opened. Deacon stood looking all nicely dressed and smiling.

"Welcome. Good to see you both together. I was worried," he said.

"Well, we have such exciting lives, it's great when we can get together." I laughed.

We went in and found Lynn sitting on the floor with the baby on a blanket. Lynn was pushing and pulling on the baby's legs.

"Are you torturing the kid?" I asked.

"Just helping to build muscle strength in her legs," Lynn replied.

"So she can walk the beat as a cop or become an exotic dancer?" I said with a smile.

"She better become neither. I'll strangle her if she does," Deacon added.

We all sat and talked about the baby and then I asked Lynn a question.

"Are you going back to work?"

She looked at the baby and was quiet. Deacon didn't say anything as Lynn pondered the question.

Network Murders

Finally she said, "I don't know yet. I still have another month on my maternity leave. If I do decide to go back, I need to be ready to be separated from the baby. It will involve finding a sitter or day care. I'm not crazy about either. I didn't realize when all this happened how it could change my life."

"Tell you what, if you don't feel you can devote all your time to the police department, maybe you could come work with us in a part-time investigative position for now."

She gave me a stare and thought on it. She looked at Deacon and then said, "That might not be a bad idea. I could work when needed and still have time for the baby."

Deacon finally spoke. "You know if you go back to the squad, you'll just get immersed in crime again. I hated to see you come home all burnt out before the baby came. I don't want that to happen again."

"Jim, I'll think on it. I've been with the police long enough to collect a small pension, but can your business take on another person? You just brought Buck on as an investigator."

"I was looking at the books earlier and we have more than enough work. Besides, Earl and Trapper take off way too much time to be called full-time employees. They treat it as fun. So you could fill in easily."

"I'll think on it," she said as she reached down for the baby and picked her up. She rocked the child and looked at Deacon. "You can take my slot as lieutenant. You deserve it."

"I'd have to pass the tests, but I think I could. We'll see what Weber has to say first. He's the biggest obstacle."

Lynn smiled and said, "I'll put the baby on his lap and threaten him to give you the position. That should do it."

*

Chapter 12

We had a nice evening visiting with Lynn, Deacon and little Penny, but it was getting late. The baby was fussing and needing to go to bed, so we decided to leave.

At the door Lynn stood and said, "Jim, I need to thank you for two important things. First for bringing Deacon out here from Michigan so I could meet him and then giving me a chance to start a new career so I can spend more time with my baby. Plus all the countless times you have helped us solve cases. Thanks again."

"Come on, sweetie, before you start getting a big head," Penny said to me.

"It was my pleasure, Lynn. You take care and take care of that baby," I said, and we went to the car.

On the way home, Penny said, "Do you think you can take on Lynn in your firm?"

Network Murders

"It's been busy lately, but she can work when she wants to. We've had to turn away a number of cases just because we've been busy. I hate to give cases to rival agencies. So I know she would fit in. Even with Buck joining us. Besides, he has his guards if we get slow."

We arrived home and I put the car away. Willy came running out of the house when Penny opened the door, so I took him for a walk. It was fall in the Valley and the night was a little nippy. I had my jacket on and it didn't bother me. Willy was scouting around for a perfect spot to relieve himself. I looked out to the lights of the strip, still amazed at its beauty. Willy was bouncing around by the house, so I figured he had enough of the cold. We went in and I found Penny in the bedroom already in bed. She never ceased to amaze me, also.

"Aren't you cold out there?" she said with the covers just under her chin. "You should get under the covers so I can warm you up." She was giving me her evil smile again.

"Why, yes, I am cold," I said and undressed in record time.

Bright and early the next morning my cell phone buzzed. I fumbled for it on the nightstand and finally knocked it to the floor. I grumbled as I swung out of bed reaching down for it.

"Hello?" I said as I answered. I didn't get to see the caller ID, my eyes hadn't focused yet.

"Jim, it's Lorelei. Sorry to wake you, but I had to ask you the name of that stripper you talked to."

I was trying to get myself up and to my bathroom while holding the phone. "Uh, her name was Molly Sharp, but she goes under the name of Candy Cane. Why?"

"They found her dead this morning, apparently from a gunshot wound."

"Where did they find her?" I asked, totally stunned.

"Behind the Golden Slipper. In the alley. Joe Lang said he'd have more for us in a while. You were going to talk to her today, weren't you?"

"I was, but that's moot now. Have you checked on Louis?"

"No, you think I should?"

"It's possible that someone didn't want Molly to say who all was at the parties, and Louis also knew. So he could be in danger too."

"I'll send a car over to check on him. If you have time to stop by the crime scene with any information you have, I'd appreciate it."

"I will. I'll be bringing Buck also."

"Okay, see you soon." She said and hung up.

"What's the matter, sweetie?" came a voice from under the covers.

"My lead witness in the killings was murdered this morning. This is heating up. I have to go to the crime scene and talk to Lorelei." I called Buck and explained to him the situation. He agreed to meet me at the office parking lot.

Penny was up and getting ready for her last local show from Vegas. After the weekend she would be back on national television. I'd have to share her again with the world.

I got ready to go, gave her a big kiss and went out to the car. I arrived at the office building and picked up Buck. He got in and I drove over to the strip club again.

"Now why would someone want to kill poor Candy?" Buck said.

"She knew who the people were who attended Isham's parties, I guess. Someone doesn't want to be exposed."

"Did Isham originally have the virus or was someone else at the party deliberately spreading it?" Buck said.

His question shook me. "Well, now that's a good question, Buck. We just assumed since Isham had the virus, he was the one spreading it. Maybe he didn't know he got it from someone else. We really need to find out who all attended the parties."

We pulled into the parking lot of the strip club and parked. Buck was already out of the car and I came out to join him.

We went around the back where there were a number of patrol cars and the ominous coroner's van. Joe Lang was just coming around the van when he saw me.

"Jim, Buck, they called you to fill in for our missing cops?" he asked with a smile.

"They don't need us getting in the way. What's the verdict on Candy?"

"She had a GSW to the head, close range, 9mm, just like Isham."

"Are you going to treat her like she had AIDS also?" I asked.

"You bet. I'm covering up real good this time. I was lucky with Isham. If I had known he had the virus, I would have been more careful. But I didn't get exposed to it."

"Question. Do you think Isham had the virus first or could he have gotten it from someone at his parties?"

"Hard to tell. He could have been a victim of someone passing it. Maybe another person who didn't know they had it."

"Or someone trying to kill a few people," Buck said.

"Very true, Buck. Someone may have had it out for the revelers," Joe said. "Lorelei is back around the corner." He went off.

Network Murders

Buck and I went around and found Lorelei standing alone by the back door. Two CSI were examining the scene when Lorelei saw us.

"Jim, what's your take?" she asked.

I explained our reason for wanting to talk to Candy about the guests at the parties. Then I mentioned Buck's theory that Isham wasn't the person spreading but a victim.

"Why was he killed if he wasn't doing the hurting?" she asked.

"Well, that's a good question too. Maybe he found out who was spreading it and wanted to expose him. The killer murdered him to shut him up. Like Candy."

"I'm getting a headache. Maybe I'm coming down with something." Lorelei smiled as she said it.

"Well, don't give it to me. Penny would kill us both. You can come to see her new show Monday if you'd like. I'll arrange it."

"Thank you, I'd like to catch a taping of her show. Especially the first national show. Do you know who her guests are?"

"I haven't paid much attention to that. I'm sure Penny knows, but she hasn't said much about it."

"Let me know where to go and I'll be there," she said.

"I'll do that. Now what have you got here?"

"As far as can be determined, she was standing by the door with her back to that wall." Lorelei pointed to a blood splattered section of the wall. "She either knew her assailant or not, but she was shot point blank from about three feet. That's the prelim from Joe. No one saw her from inside, no one told her to come out here."

"Did she have a cell phone?" I asked.

Lorelei looked to the lead CSI and asked. He brought a bag over with a cell phone and handed it to her while he waited. Lorelei looked at it and pushed buttons through the bag. "She had a call from just before Joe said she was killed. I'll have the number checked, but it's probably a burn phone. That may be how she was called out."

"If so, then whoever it was knew her and her number. I'm betting on someone from the parties. We really need to talk to Louis and see who all was attending."

"I had a car go by there but he wasn't in. I have a BOLO out for him."

*

Chapter 13

"Isham and Candy are dead and Glass doesn't know anything, so we need Louis to tell us who else attended those parties. Before the virus gets spread further. And maybe find out who started the virus spread," I said.

Network Murders

Joe Lang came back around the side of the building with his assistants. They were pulling the gurney to put the body bag on. I stood back while they lifted it and took it away.

"That's one thing that has bothered me about this business. I talk to a person one day and the next they are gone from this world. Sad," I said.

My cell phone buzzed and I stepped aside to answer. Caller ID said it was Angelo. "Hey, big guy, what's up?"

"I talked to my lady friend and she's coming in for dinner tonight. Sorry for the short notice, but she's a busy woman. Can you and the Mrs. make it?"

"Nothing will keep us away, Angelo. What time?"

"Seven will be fine for you to come. I'm cooking the dinner myself, so you may need to entertain her, if you would."

"My pleasure, and I'm sure Penny will get along fine with her." I hope, I thought. "We'll be there just before seven. See you then."

"Thanks, Mr. R, I appreciate it." He hung up.

I called Penny to connect with her on this. She came on quickly and said, "What's up, sweetie?"

"I got a call from Angelo. He apologized for the late notice, but he'd like us to meet his lady friend tonight at seven. You good with that?"

"Have you decided if she is good for Angelo?"

"I couldn't find anything wrong with her, so she's good. Now are you good with going?"

"I'll be glad to meet her. I'll be ready when you are," she said and hung up.

I smiled and put my phone away then went back to Lorelei and Buck. They were talking about Buck's background. I didn't want to tarnish his bad boy past so I just listened.

"You never ran with a biker club?" Lorelei asked.

"No, I was a loner. A king of the road. I didn't answer to anyone," he said, puffing out his chest. I was waiting for him to beat his chest like a rogue gorilla. I had to laugh to myself.

Buck looked at me and asked, "Anything important?"

"Just a dinner date with Penny. So have you two solved the case yet?"

"Nope, we've been comparing notes on Sando. Seems he's a nasty customer," Buck said, sounding official.

"I got that opinion when we met him. Lorelei, if you hear anything on finding Louis, let me know please," I requested.

"I'll do that. If you pick up any info, let me know," she requested.

I nodded, looked at Buck and said, "Shall we head out?"

We walked out past the death wagon just pulling out with poor Candy's body. Had she known more than was healthy for her? Or maybe she stiffed a customer and he didn't like it. Although Candy did say she was bi. Maybe it was a woman who murdered her. Either way she was dead and we weren't any closer to finding out anything. Louis was our hope now to find others who might have attended the orgies.

We got into the car and I sat a moment gathering my thoughts.

"Where to now?" Buck asked.

"I have no idea. Don't you just love investigating? We need Louis and he's not around. Maybe if we go by the condos, we could find him."

"I'm game. Shall we go?"

I drove back to the condos where Lorelei and I met Louis. Buck and I got out and we walked around the lot, looking at the building.

"Maybe if we talk to some of the neighbors, they might be helpful," I said.

"You are good at this investigating," he said with a grin.

"And you are a wise-ass," I replied and walked to the condo next to Isham's.

I knocked at the door and waited. After a few moments the door opened and there stood an older woman who looked to be in her seventies, I presumed. She looked good and had a vitality about her, but I could tell she had seen better days.

"May I help you gentlemen?" she asked, then eyed Buck with a bit of apprehension.

"Don't worry, ma'am, he doesn't bite. I'm Jim Richards and this is my associate Buck Carson. We're private investigators investigating the murder of Percy Isham."

"So tragic. He was a very nice man and so polite. I can't believe someone would do him in. Do you have any leads so far?" she said, sounding like she watched too many crime shows.

"We're working on it. What can you tell me about the parties Isham used to throw?"

"Oh, I didn't pay much attention. They didn't bother me. It's hard to hear through the walls in this building so they were never loud enough to disturb me."

"Did you possibly see anyone who attended?"

"Well, I wasn't nosy, but there were a number of beautiful people. No one I knew, but that one man…I'm sure he was a reporter for a local station. He gave the news, Tim something."

"Tim Lineman?"

Network Murders

"Yes, I'm sure that's his name. I saw him a couple times. He always had a beautiful woman on his arm. I never knew what went on during those parties, but Louis would tell me they were wild. Too bad I was never asked to attend," she said with a grin at Buck. He shifted away from her a little.

"Do you happen to know where Louis is?"

"The police asked me that earlier. I don't really know. Is he a suspect?"

"Everyone is a suspect at this point. Even you since Isham never asked you to attend his parties. Maybe that angered you?"

She broke out laughing. "No, you sweet thing. I'm not the killing type. Least of all with a gun. I'd poison him with my homemade cookies. I make great cookies. Would you like some?"

"Not after that comment, but thanks. If you see Louis, could you call me right away?" I said handing her my card.

"I'll do that." She smiled and went back into her house.

"That lady looks dangerous," Buck said as we walked back to the parking lot.

We stood by my car as I watched the condos. Some curtains were moving, which told me people there liked to watch their neighbors.

"Let's try the neighbor on the other side of Isham." We went to the door and it opened before I could knock. It was a younger man in his thirties, I would say.

"Are you cops?" the man asked.

"No sir, we're private investigators. What do you know about Percy Isham?" I asked.

"The man was a pig. He always had people coming and going, sweaty people. People who lusted for what Isham gave."

"And that was?"

"Drugs. Of course they were into drugs. I know because I saw those drug lords coming to his door with their illegal goods. I told the cops that and they noted it. I don't think they'll do anything because of that cop Isham was involved with."

"Cop?" I remembered Candy telling me about a cop. He could be the one who murdered her.

"Yeah, he would come in a patrol car sometimes, and they would stand by the door arguing about money. Seems Isham owed some people money for something, but they didn't say who."

"You heard this?"

"Well, my easy chair is next to the front window and I have good hearing. The cop threatened him once with harm. But that was a while back. Does this help?"

"Very much so. Did you happen to see who attended the parties?"

"I don't know any of the people. Louis would know. He always hung around in the room with them."

"Do you know where Louis might be right now?"

"He could be anywhere. He's into illegal things too, so he keeps low."

"What kind of illegal things?"

"I think he was into numbers and hooked to the mob."

Now I was wondering about this guy. "Why do you say that?"

"I saw Louis out in the parking lot a couple times talking to someone in a black limo. They probably were in the mob."

"I don't suppose you got the license plate number," I asked.

"Hey, I do my best to help the law. Of course I did." He went back into the room and returned with a piece of paper. I looked at it and it was a plate number.

"Thank you. If you see Louis let me know," I said handing him my card.

"I will and I won't alert him that you want him."

"That would be a big help. We just need to question him." I looked at Buck and said with a grin, "Shall we go investigate these new facts?"

"Most certainly," Buck replied.

"Thank you, sir, you've been very helpful," I said to the man.

"My name is Buzz Lightyear, remember that name. I'll be famous one day," he said with a big smile. I think he believed himself.

Buck and I left Buzz alone and went to the car again.

"Now that man needs some help," Buck said.

"I think he may be crazy but he may have given us some good leads. Even with his delusions, he had to see things. This plate number may help. I'll call Lorelei and see what she can find out about this and the mysterious cop."

*

Chapter 14

We sat in my car as I called Lorelei. "Got some things for you that may help." I explained our adventures at the condos with the loony neighbors.

"Give me the plate number and I'll run it," Lorelei said. "Who is the cop that was harassing Isham?"

Network Murders

"I was told by Candy his name was Nate. Or so she heard. Not a real common name. Should be easy to find."

"Already found it. Nathan Bartan, known by his buddies as Nate. He works the Drug Task Force and has access to numerous dealers, pushers and users."

"Well, that sounds reasonable to assume he's our man. Do you know where he is?" I asked.

"Yeah, I'm looking at him. He's in the squad room talking to one of my men. I swear if I have bad cops in my squad I'll hang them by the testicles."

"Ouch. Can you hang on to him so I can come in to watch you question him?"

"I'll even let you do some questioning. Get in here and I'll try to hang on to him."

"I'm on my way," I said and hung up. I looked at Buck and said, "Shall we go bar-b-que a cop?"

"I'll just watch. I'm not into cop burgers." He laughed and I started the car and drove out.

We arrived shortly afterward and went in. Lorelei had moved back into Lynn's squad since Lynn and Deacon were off. I was surprised they didn't call Deacon back in since they were short of people due to the flu.

"Why didn't they call Deacon back in?" I asked when Lorelei appeared.

"Weber doesn't want him getting sick and infecting the baby. I think Weber cares way too much for the child," she said.

"Nothing wrong with that. Now, did you manage to detain Nate?"

"I had to twist his arm and threaten him with arrest. But he's sitting quietly in Interrogation Two. I got a guard on the door just in case." She smiled and headed to the room. Buck and I followed. I pointed to the observation room for Buck and he went there.

Lorelei asked, "Are you ready?"

"Always," I replied.

"Bartan is a cop, so he knows you don't mean diddle in there. You're just a consultant helping to observe and add questions. But if he gets nasty, you'll have to back off."

"Hey, I'm on the roster as an auxiliary cop. I'm almost official," I defended.

"Well, then you can beat the hell out of him and I'll look away." She grinned and opened the door. We went in.

"What the hell, Paris? Why am I sitting in this box when I should be out on the street?" he barked.

"I have a few questions to ask you in regards to a murder I'm investigating. So sit back and enjoy your short vacation from crime."

Network Murders

She sat across from him and I stood behind her. Bartan looked at me and frowned.

"You're that annoying P.I. Richards, aren't you? The one who helped put Steve Duffey in the ground."

I saw Lorelei stiffen. Duffey was the vigilante cop who was caught and killed. Her boyfriend was Duffey's brother. I should say, ex-boyfriend.

"Duffey was a bad cop, misguided in his mission, but still a bad cop," Lorelei said. "Are you a bad cop? I have a witness who says that you were harassing my victim before he was murdered."

"What the hell you talking about? I don't know from any murders. Who you talking about?"

"Percy Isham. Sound familiar?"

Bartan shut up and sat back. Then, "I don't know any Percy what's-his-name. You got nothing."

I spoke. "I have a witness who saw you arguing with Isham and even threatening him. Something about money owed to someone. Maybe a bookie? Are you collecting for a bookie?"

"Hey, I'm in Drugs, not Vice. Talk to them."

"Doesn't matter what squad you work in, you can still go out and collect for a bookie. Come on, Nate, fess up and make my life easier," Lorelei said.

"I got nothing to say. I don't know any Isham and I didn't kill anybody."

"Bartan, I'm just questioning you now, but I may want to put you in a line up for our witness. Don't go anywhere," Lorelei said.

Lorelei stood and went out. I followed. Buck came out of observation and over to us. Bartan left the room and quickly went out of the squad room.

"I think you should put a watch on the crazy neighbor even if Bartan doesn't know who we were talking about. He may figure it out."

"Good idea." She called over to Warren and explained the situation. Warren said he was on it and left after I explained who he was watching. I also warned him about the nutjob's delusions.

I could hear Warren calling out from the hallway, "To infinity and beyond," and a loud laugh.

Buck said, "I like Warren, but he's a strange man."

"He doesn't take all this seriously," I said. "Which is why I like him too." I turned to Lorelei and asked, "Have you gotten a hit on the plates?"

"Not yet. I'll call and set a fire under someone." She went off and made a call from her desk.

I turned to Buck. "Bartan is probably a bag man for the bookies. As I always say, it's stupid for a bookie to kill a debtor. You can't collect from a dead man."

Network Murders

"We could talk to Angelo about his experiences with collecting money," Buck replied. "Maybe get some insight on what they do short of murder."

"This happened in Isham's office. It was quiet there and no one else around to witness the murder. A perfect way to kill someone. I think this goes beyond gambling debts. I'm still going with the AIDS problem being the cause of his death. We need a list of people attending the parties."

"Which means we need Louis," Buck said.

"I'm going to follow up on that one guest, Tim Lineman, the news guy. He's from Penny's station, so she might help me pin him down."

Lorelei came back and said, "Well, the plates are registered to Springhill Management. They own the condos that people like Isham lease. Probably Louis was just talking to his boss about some problem in the complex."

"I would think a phone call would suffice rather than a visit. But who knows what the managers feel like doing. Take a ride in a limo just to talk to the super," I said.

"They have a misguided sense of worth, I would say," Lorelei said with a smile.

"We have another lead I want to follow up on. I haven't mentioned it to you since I didn't know if it would pan out. I don't want to waste your valuable time here."

"If it's something that will get me away from here, fine. What do you have?" she asked.

"The woman neighbor said she thought she saw Tim Lineman, the news anchor, going into the party. He works for Penny's studio so I thought we'd go talk to him. If you want to go, you're more than welcome."

She thought on it then said, "I'll pass, but let me know what you find. Weber is keeping me busy enough with paperwork. It's not helping to solve crimes but without the paperwork these bad guys could go free in the courts."

"Well, you keep our streets safe with your files. I'll call if I find anything. Oh, do you want me to talk to Buzz Lightyear about coming in to view a lineup?"

She laughed then said, "Yeah, see what he says and if he'll cooperate. Thanks."

Buck and I went out of the building and to the car. Buck asked, "Are we going to visit Buzz first or to the studio?"

I stopped by the car and said, "Buzz is closer, then the studio." I got in the car and we drove out.

We arrived at the condos again and I parked away from Isham's place. I didn't want Buzz to see us just yet. I got out and looked around the lot for Warren. I saw him getting out of his car across the lot and he came to me.

"So what's happening?" I asked him.

Network Murders

"Buzz Lightyear is in his apartment," he said with a giggle. "I talked to him earlier and he agreed to participate with a lineup. So far it's been quiet here. No attempts on him yet."

We both stood and looked towards Buzz's condo. We watched for a moment when we saw a car drive in and park in front of Buzz's place.

"Crap, that looks like Bartan," Warren said.

"Yes, he does. Let's wait and see what he does," I said.

Bartan got out of the car and looked around the lot. Buck, Warren and I ducked down to avoid being seen. We carefully looked through the windows of the car we were hiding behind and saw him go to the door. He looked around again and then knocked.

"I don't think we should give him time to kill Buzz. Let's move," I said.

We ran along the back of the cars in the lot until we were right across from Buzz's door. He hadn't answered yet, and Bartan stood waiting. I could see Bartan had his gun behind his back and told Warren. Warren stood, went towards Bartan with his service weapon out front and yelled, "Bartan, drop the gun, now!"

Bartan turned with a shocked look on his face. He brought up his gun and before he could fire, Warren dropped him.

*

Chapter 15

We ran to Bartan on the ground. He was moving so he was alive. Warren checked him and said, "I hit him in the shoulder, he'll live." He pulled out his cell phone and made a call.

Fifteen minutes later there was a flurry of activity. Mainly because a cop was shot. Lorelei was heading the circus, talking to Warren.

"So we need to get this under control. There's going to be a number of angry cops wanting to know what happened here." She yelled to Williams who had just arrived and told him to have Bartan taken into custody, read him his rights and be sure he went to the hospital with police protection.

"Don't let anyone near him until I can talk to him and call IAB in on this. They will want to get their hooks into this. Move quickly before the trouble gets worse."

Captain Weber came up to us and said, "Explain to me why a cop was shot by one of my squad."

Lorelei explained the events up to Warren shooting Bartan. He stood thinking and then said, "Good work. Get Bartan in official custody and be sure to dot the i's and cross the t's. I want this bad cop to go down." He turned and went off.

"He hasn't changed. Hit and run," I said with a laugh. "So this doesn't solve who killed Isham, but it brings us closer. I really think it's the AIDS thing, but the gambling aspect could be the cause. I still need to talk to Lineman to see who were the guests at the parties."

"I have to tie things up here. I have a ton of questions to answer with IAB, but you can go. Let me know what you find."

"I will. Good luck with the vultures," I said and pulled Buck towards the car.

We got in and I drove out. "Doesn't this show that Bartan could have killed Isham?" Buck asked.

"Forensic will determine if the gun used by Bartan is the gun that killed Isham. But I'll say again, it doesn't fit. Unless Bartan had something else going on with Isham, he wouldn't kill him."

"I know, dead men don't pay debts," Buck said with a laugh.

"You're learning, grasshopper." I pulled into the studio parking lot and into a space.

"Is Penny still here?" Buck asked.

"She should be just finishing her last local show. Monday she goes back to national. Are you going to bring Maria?"

"If she can make it, I will. Either way, I'll be there. It should be fun," Buck said.

"Yes, it will. I think Penny is really looking forward to this. She loves the attention. I've seen it every time we are out and someone recognizes her. She eats it up."

I parked and we went in. The security guard at the door recognized Buck and me and let us pass. We walked down the hallway to Penny's studio and to her dressing room. I looked in and there were her "groupies" as she called them. The women who dressed her and made up her face and hair. They saw me and cheered.

Buck and I entered, and the women went straight for Buck. He had that effect on women. They had the monitor on in the room for Penny's show. Penny looked great. She was really milking the crowd.

"Okay, people, this is my last local show from Las Vegas. I'm still going to be here but the show will now be seen across the nation. So you can come down and be seen by millions of viewers. Okay, maybe not millions but a whole lot of people."

The audience laughed and clapped.

"Monday at eleven o'clock this show will be seen on the CW network and broadcast across the country. So tune in and see our great guests, actress Patsy Harper and TV hunk Darius Curling from the show, "LA Underground." We will have the rock group, Twinkle, performing on the new arena stage just outside this building. It will be a concert you'll want to see. So I say with much sadness, good-bye for now and see you Monday." She finished while the music played, shaking hands with the audience, and then the show went black. The monitor shut down and

113

Network Murders

I turned to see the women and Buck watching. They cheered and then Penny came storming into the room.

"Sweetie!" she yelled. "You made it." She threw her arms around me.

"Now, would I miss your last show?" I said, afraid to mention about Lineman. I'd wait for a bit until she settled.

She sat in the chair while her girls worked on her to remove the stage make-up and put her daily face back on. They were quick and soon had her back to the woman I had to deal with every day.

"I'm so excited. I don't know if I can wait until Monday," she said. "We need to celebrate. Are we still going to Angelo's to meet his hot woman?"

"So far as I know, it's still on. I do have one small favor to ask," I said as she stood, changed to my wife again.

"Sure, what?" she said.

"I need to talk to Tim Lineman. Do you know him well enough to arrange that?"

"Tim? Sure, he's in the studio. Do you need to talk to him now?"

"The sooner the better. It could be a matter of his health," I said.

She gave me a look and then said, "Okay, you need to explain first before I turn you loose on him."

I took her out into the hallway, away from Buck and the women. I gave her a kiss and she said, "Don't think that's going to get you any favors. Now talk."

I explained the details of the case that she didn't know already. I finished and said, "So I need to talk to Lineman to warn him about the AIDS and find out who else may have been at the parties."

"AIDS is nothing to sneeze at. I'll see where Tim is and we can go talk to him." She kissed me back and said, "Let's get this done."

She turned and went down the hallway. I followed. Buck stuck his head out of the dressing room and I said to follow.

We went through the mess of people running around getting shows ready to tape or go live. Soon the network would be intruding on the studio to tape Penny's show. It would be another mess, but a good one.

We went through a double door marked Studio C and into the newsroom. A number of the crew were working to get the place ready for the day's hot newsbreaks. I could see Lineman standing at the news desk along with Helen Morgan, his co-anchor, and Tracey Wilson the weather girl.

"Penny!" came a voice from behind the lights. It was a man I had met before. The director of the news programing, Frank Lawson.

He came over and hugged Penny then looked at me. "Hey, did you have to bring your husband?"

Network Murders

"He's kind of part of the team. So I need to talk to Tim, if Mr. Wonderful can tear himself away from the news desk."

"I'll get him. We have about twenty minutes before the afternoon news, so don't talk too long."

"We'll be brief," I said. "Promise."

"Okay," he said and yelled to Lineman. "Timmy, come here now."

Lineman put his papers down and came to us.

"Penny, good to see you. How's it feel to be back in the limelight?"

"Good. Can we talk?" she said.

"Uh, sure. Is it important?" he asked.

"It could be real important to you. Let's go into one of the rehearsal rooms." She led him to one of the rooms on the side where people would run their lines alone.

I closed the door behind me when Lineman, Penny, Buck and I were in the room.

He looked at me and said, "You're Penny's husband, Jim Richards."

"Yes, I am and, as you know, I'm a private investigator."

Bob Moats

"Sure, I've covered your adventures in Vegas. You're quite a cowboy," he said.

"Well, yippee ki yo ki yay. I have to talk to you about Percy Isham."

He suddenly looked shocked and shut up. Then, "What about him?"

"I'm sure you know he's dead. He was murdered Wednesday night in his office. But that's not what I need to ask you. First, did you know Percy had AIDS?"

Lineman suddenly went limp and sat on a chair in the room. He looked pale and said, "How do you know?"

"The coroner who autopsied his body confirmed it. What I need to know is who all attended the parties he held. It's important that everyone knows about this."

"Jesus, I haven't any idea who all was at his party. I can give you a couple names but not everyone. Damn, this isn't good. Should I be concerned?"

"If you had sex with any of his partners, you should," I said.

He was silent for a short while. Penny, Buck and I waited.

"Damn, just when I thought it was safe to go back to an orgy…I'll give you what I know. But there were a lot of people at those parties. If they have the virus, it will be spread if they are having sex elsewhere. How do we reach them?"

117

"Let's start with the people you know. They may know others," I said.

Penny spoke. "Why don't you do a news report about Isham's death and mention he was found to have AIDS? It might bring in a good number of people who are concerned."

I looked at my wife and then gave her a big kiss. "I knew you were good for something."

*

Chapter 16

Lineman rushed out of the room, followed by us.

"What's he up to?" Buck asked.

"I hope something good," I replied.

"He's going to see Frank Lawson, I'll bet," Penny said.

Lineman went into the news control booth and was talking to Lawson. They seemed to be having a minor debate about something, then Lineman went to another desk and wrote something on a paper. He stood, went to another man and handed him the sheet. The man read it and looked at Lineman with a bit of surprise. Then the man typed on his keyboard as the words came up on a monitor. I realized it was the teleprompter that they read the news from. I couldn't read it from where I stood, but I hoped Lineman was doing justice to the story.

He came back to us and said, "I talked Frank into going top story with this. It's a warning, an important warning. After this broadcast I'm heading in to my doctor to get checked. Thank you for the information." He left the room and went to get his make-up on. He sat at the news desk and got ready for broadcast, as the make-up girl had finished putting the final touches on him before leaving. The stage director called to everyone to be ready.

I watched on a monitor for the show to start. Buck and Penny were beside me, gazes glued to the screen.

The opening credits scrolled by as the music blurb played and the announcer brought the show to a start. Then the camera went to Lineman.

"Good evening, Las Vegas. On our top story this day we have a report that must be heard. Two days ago a studio head for the CW network, Percy Isham, was murdered in his Las Vegas office late at night. Police are still investigating the crime. It has been reported to me by very reliable sources that Isham was a victim of the AIDS virus and had frequent physical contact with other persons unknown. If you have had or know anyone who has had contact with Isham, you are advised to contact a doctor for testing."

Lineman went on for a brief explanation of the crime and a request that anyone who had information about the crime should contact the police. Then he went on to other news.

I heard Penny exhale. She had held her breath during the news bit. "Well, that should help your investigation. Now you won't have to worry about finding all the people involved in the orgy."

"Yes, and now that it has been reported, the other media will pick up on this and spread the word even more," I said.

"Sure, it's salacious news. Big exec had AIDS and could have infected others. The media will eat it up," Buck said.

"Sad but true, Buck. At least people have been warned." I looked at Penny. "Don't we have a dinner date?"

"Ow! I almost forgot. Angelo and his gold digger lady friend."

"Hey, I cleared her of any misdemeanors and she's probably a very nice person. Just what Angelo needs. Now let's go get ready," I said.

I dropped Buck off at his car and drove out to go home. I called Lorelei on the way and told her about the news report. She said it should help, and that Bartan was not cooperating. Internal Affairs was questioning him also but not getting cooperation either.

"Bartan is going to suffer badly if he gets put in lockup with the cons who hate cops. So I think he may want to cut a deal and give up his bookie friends," she said.

"Whatever. Have you heard from Louis yet?"

"Nope, he's still hiding out. Makes me wonder what he's up to."

"Well, keep me informed. I have an important dinner to go to tonight so no calls until late."

"I'll keep it in mind, talk later," she said, then hung up.

I arrived at home. Penny was already cleaning up and was picking out a dress. That would take a while.

"What time do we meet them?" she asked.

"Angelo said seven, which gives us two hours. What do you want to do until then? We could fool around."

"You can fool around with yourself. I'm going to take a quick nap and you are not allowed to join me. I'll never get to sleep."

I laughed and said, "I'll go work on my book. I'm almost finished with it."

"Which one is this?"

"The one about the Elvis murders. I'm making it into a comedy," I said.

"Just don't mention my distaste for Elvis. I have an image to maintain." She pushed me out of the bedroom and closed the door.

Network Murders

I just smiled and went to my home office.

Around six-thirty we were both ready to go to dinner. Willy was fed and resting happily on his blanket we gave him to sleep on in the kitchen while we were out. We decided to use Penny's car so she could be the designated driver. I was sure I'd need a few beers to get through the night.

We arrived at the restaurant and parked. Angelo was at the door greeting people and saw us. He gushed and thanked us for coming.

"She's not here yet. She called and said she was on her way. I'll seat you and get some drinks on the house." He signaled to his waitress and she came to take us to a good table by the fireplace. We gave the girl our drink orders and she went off.

"Not a good sign to be late," Penny said.

"I'm sure she has a good reason. You know I was the skeptical one at first. Now you are being a little snippy about this."

"I know, I'm sorry. This is Angelo, our friend, and I want him to be happy," she said.

"Well, he looks happy to me," I said as I watched him moving around the room, talking with customers. Then he stopped and excused himself, going to the front entrance. I couldn't see who he was talking to but he came into the room with an attractive woman dressed in a cocktail dress and looking very refined. An odd match for Angelo's rough exterior.

He brought the woman to our table. I stood.

"Mr. and Mrs. R, this is Sophia." He beamed with pride. I thought he was going to burst, but he held up well.

"Sophia, pleasure to meet you. I'm Jim Richards," I said, holding my hand out. "This is my wife and TV host, Penny Wickens-Richards."

"Yes, I know both of you, and I must say I'm honored to meet you. Angie has said so many good things about the both of you. I feel I know you already."

Angie? I thought it was cute, but I would never call him Angie. It was her pet name for him and she could keep it.

Angelo pulled her seat out for her and they exchanged a quick kiss. I sat, and then Angelo said, "I'm going to get your dinner ready. It's a special treat, an old family recipe. I'll be back." He went off and I looked at Sophia.

"So you are in the restaurant business also?" I asked.

"Well, the end that provides equipment to restaurants. I met Angelo at a restaurant trade show and arranged to talk to him about some new equipment. He didn't tell me all his equipment is new. He wanted to meet me again. I was flattered, and we've been seeing each other now for about three weeks."

Penny asked, "Do you and Angelo talk about each other much?"

Network Murders

"If you're asking if I know about Angelo's past, I do. It doesn't bother me. I have a few relatives that are a little sketchy, but I don't judge. Angelo is his own man and not in the family business anymore."

"Angelo has been an upstanding citizen since he has moved here from New York," I said. "He worked for my firm as a bodyguard and had always wanted a restaurant, so we got him into one. He's a legitimate businessman now."

"And he's a doll. I've never met a more polite or caring man than him. I think that is why I was attracted to him. I'm sure you're concerned for your friend, but be assured I would never do anything to hurt him."

I was starting to like her. Penny was still on the fence judging from her facial expressions. But she smiled finally.

We talked about everything related to Angelo. I told her a few tales about his adventures in body guarding and how we met Angelo.

Angelo would come by our table every so often to check on us and then skitter back to the kitchen.

"Have you had any meals prepared by Angelo?" Penny asked.

"Oh yes, he is such a good chef. I love his Italian foods. I'm Italian myself. My family came over when I was very young. I was born in Palermo. Most of my family still speak the language. Which made Angelo very happy when he met them last week. They talked in Italian the whole time we visited."

Now that was something I never thought about. Angelo spoke Italian. I knew he was Italian, but it never occurred to me that he spoke it.

Angelo came back with two waitresses and trays of food. The waitresses set out the meals as Angelo, now dressed in a suit, sat next to Sophia.

After the waitresses had finished setting out the food, Angelo stood, held up one of the glasses of wine that had been brought to our table and made a toast.

"To my good friends," he said, pointing his glass to Penny and me then to Sophia, "and a new close friend. May we always be together and family."

*

Chapter 17

We finished our dinner. It was fabulous, the best Angelo had ever made. Probably to impress his lady friend. But we enjoyed it also.

"Angelo, you outdid yourself with that meal," I said.

Network Murders

"Thanks, Mr. R, it was one of my mother's favorite recipes. By the way, Mom is coming out Sunday. She wants to be in the audience for Penny's new show."

Penny made a little squeal and said, "Great, it will be so good to see Frances again. How is she coming?"

"On the family jet to McCarran. I have to meet her by ten in the morning."

"Well, Angelo, you'll need the mini-limo to pick her up. I'll come by your place and pick you up by nine-thirty," I said.

"Me too, I'm coming," Penny said happily.

"I hope you don't mind, I asked Sophia to come also. Mom wants to meet her," Angelo said.

"Of course, the limo will hold all of us. I'll drive," I said.

"That's real nice of you, Mr. R. It will be good to see Mom again."

We talked a bit more and the evening was wearing on. I gave our excuses to leave and we thanked Angelo for the food and the company.

"So good meeting you, Sophia. We, of course, will be seeing each other more often. So take care," I said.

Penny said her good-byes and we went out to the car. I hadn't drunk much so I drove back to the house.

126

"Okay, she's a nice woman," Penny said. "I approve."

"That's very nice of you to approve. I'm sure Angelo will be happy to hear that." I smiled at the thought.

"It will be nice to see Frances again. It's been way too long."

"It's always nice to have a mob family matriarch at your show premiere. It makes you respectable."

"I just hope the FBI doesn't hide in the audience watching her," Penny said with a smirk.

"I don't think they worry about the women of the family. Now if Gino came to the show there would be Feebies all over the place," I said.

I pulled into the drive and put the car in the garage. We went into the kitchen and I reset the driveway alarm. Willy was bouncing all over the place.

"Damn, we forgot to bring Willy home a doggy bag," I said.

Penny laughed and pulled out a small bag from her huge purse. "Angelo slipped it to me when you went to get our coats."

I laughed. "Very thoughtful of him," I said.

She dished out the food into Willy's bowl as I went into the living room after grabbing a couple beers for us. Penny came out and plopped down next to me.

Network Murders

"That was a fun night, and she's just fine with me," Penny affirmed again.

"Glad you approve. Now shall we watch TV and vegetate?"

"I'm for that," Penny said and opened another bag of chips from the box she had sent to us from Michigan. My favorite, Better Made Chips. We watched the idiot box and then went to bed.

Early the next morning we were resting in bed. It was Saturday and I wanted to just stay in bed and not think about crime.

Penny was snoring softly as I watched Willy sleeping next to my head. He looked content. I suddenly had to use the bathroom, so carefully moved Willy above my head and slid out of the bed. I picked up my cell phone from the night stand like I always did when I got out of bed. I hated to be in the bathroom if my phone suddenly rang in the other room.

I did my business and sat for a moment longer, almost falling back to sleep. I looked at the clock on the bathroom wall which I usually didn't do in the morning. It said six. I finished up the paperwork and stood just as my cell phone buzzed.

I looked at the caller ID. It was Lorelei. I remembered when Deacon or Lynn would wake me that early. I answered.

"You're lucky I was awake," I said into the phone.

"Sorry, but you told me to tell you when we found Louis," she said.

"Well, that's okay. What's happening?" I asked.

"Louis returned this morning about five and we nabbed him. He said he went to visit his sister in Kingman. We checked and he was there. I got him cooling his heels in lockup. I'm going to question him in a couple hours after he stews about being arrested as a material witness. I figured you'd want to be there."

"Yes, I do. What time exactly?"

"Nine o'clock too early for you?"

"No, I'll be there. Thanks," I said and hung up. I called Buck. He had to learn about being called early in the morning on these things. He wasn't happy, but I reminded him he was now a P.I. and had to be available.

"I got very little sleep with the guards. Now I have to be on call all day in case of a thug pull in. Do I really need to be included in the questioning? It's Saturday, man."

I tried not to laugh. Buck had worked hard for his guards and spent many sleepless hours covering for them. "Buck, it's not crucial that you have to be there. So you go back to sleep and I'll talk to you later." I heard him say thanks and we finished.

I looked at myself in the bathroom mirror and thought about going on a diet. That lasted about three seconds. I went back to bed and set my alarm for eight o'clock. Penny mumbled something about my bouncing on the bed. I slipped back in and tried to sleep. Visions of Louis swam through my head as I wondered what was going to come from that. We already took a step to warning the party goers about the AIDS, but we needed to know who all attended. They all were suspects.

I must have fallen asleep because I was awakened by the alarm. I hit the kill button and sat up, looked back and Penny was gone.

I stood, went into my bathroom again and got ready for the day. I came out to the kitchen and found Penny at the snack bar eating her usual oatmeal.

"Why are you getting up so early?" I asked.

"I just feel like it. I guess I'm getting antsy about the show Monday. I should just sleep through the whole weekend, but I can't. So what are you up to?"

"I'm going to watch while our witness is questioned about Isham's parties. Maybe get some info on who attended the sex parties," I said.

She ate down the last of her mush, stood and said, "I'll be ready in ten minutes. You'd better wait for me."

Before I could protest, she went to her bathroom. Oh, well, I thought, couldn't hurt to have her along. She was good at coming up with ideas.

Ten minutes later on the dot, she came out and picked up Willy, putting him in his carry bag.

"You're taking the dog, too?" I asked.

"Yes, we have been neglecting him too much. He needs to get out on our adventures, too."

"Fine, we need to go," I said as I turned her toward the garage door and out to the Crown Vic. I drove out and to the precinct. The guard at the door smiled and let us pass.

"Who's doing the questioning?" Penny asked.

I was hesitant, but said, "Lorelei."

"Oh, goody, your girlfriend."

"Knock that off. She's the primary investigator on this, so she's going to question him," I said as we entered the squad room.

Lorelei was talking to Warren when she saw us. "Penny! So good to see you. Are you ready for your show?"

Penny perked up and said, "I am having fits waiting for Monday to get here. Will you be able to come?"

"I'll be there unless there's another murder. We've had two already and I'm hoping that's all."

I had to interrupt before they started yakking. "So you have Louis?"

"Oh yes, he's in room three waiting. Feel like joining me?" she asked.

"Sure. Is he ready to be interrogated?"

She smiled and said, "Penny, are you going to watch your hubby tear into this creep?"

"I'll laugh all the way through it."

I glared and turned her to the observation room. I opened the door and pushed her in. I could hear her protesting as I closed the door. Lorelei was laughing.

"Let's get into Louis' face," she said and went to the door.

We entered, and Louis tried to jump up but his handcuffs were attached to the table and he didn't get very high. He fell back down and wailed, "What is going on? Why am I here?"

"Louis, calm down and relax. We need to know what you know." Lorelei sat across from him. I sat on the side chair.

"Louis, you know that Isham had frequent parties. Sex parties. Do you know who all attended?" Lorelei asked.

"I know most of them, yes. Why?"

"Did you know that Isham had AIDS?"

Louis was silent, looking stunned.

"Close your mouth and then think real hard on the names of the guests."

"I was arrested for that?" he asked.

132

"No, you are a suspect in this also. If you want to clear yourself, help us find the people who attended so we can find the real killer."

Louis was silent again. I could see his wheels turning. "Okay, but can I get out of these?" he asked, bringing his hands up and clanging the cuffs.

Lorelei pulled a key from her pocket and released him. Louis rubbed his wrists then made a break for the door.

I clocked him in the head before he got out. I bent down to him on the ground and said, "That was stupid."

*

Chapter 18

I pulled him up from the floor and sat him back in his chair. I brought my chair between him and the door. "Try it again, dummy," I said.

He just sat there rubbing his head. "I should sue you for attacking me."

Lorelei leaned forward and said, "Louis, wise up, you have no legal standing to sue. You attempted to escape from us. We could put you away for that. Now just help us. That's all we ask. We'll cooperate with you."

"I'm just the building super. I fix things when they get broke. I did get to know the people at the parties, sure. They were all drunk and open about who they were. I didn't know about the AIDS thing, honestly. If I had, I wouldn't have hung around. Geez, I don't need that."

"Okay, Louis, I'm going to have you write down the names of the people and where they can be reached if you know. Be honest and maybe we'll catch a killer," Lorelei said.

"You think someone from the parties killed Isham?" Louis said.

"We don't know until we rule out a few people. Now write," she said as she pushed a pad of paper and a pencil towards him.

I stood and pointed to the door. Lorelei nodded and I went out. I called to Warren at his desk and told him about Louis trying to escape. He said he'd watch him and went in the room.

I went to observation and sat next to Penny and Willy.

"I thought you were so forceful in there. Taking down the creep. I'll have to reward you later," Penny said with a smirk.

"I'll look forward to it," I said as I watched Lorelei and Warren watching Louis writing on the pad. "He's a scum. I don't know if I would trust him with the names. But then, if he wants off the suspect list, he should be truthful."

Louis was writing feverishly. He stopped and looked at his list then handed it back to Lorelei. She looked at it and said something to Warren then she stood, heading to the door.

"Hey, I cooperated, now can I go?" Louis' voice came through the speakers in our room, recording the whole thing.

"Just relax, and after we see if you gave us good information, we'll consider it." She turned and went out. Louis was still complaining. Warren pulled him up and took him out of the room. I presumed back to his cell.

Penny said, "Is that all there is? That isn't like on TV where they brow beat the suspect and spend an hour dragging information from him."

"Sometimes you just got to get to the heart of the matter, and they usually cooperate. If you threaten them just right."

"I like fake shows better. This is boring other than the attempted escape and you stopping him. That was exciting," she said.

"Yeah, well, I felt the muscle pains in my body after I moved too quickly. Now I'll need a massage to iron out the kinks."

"Dream on. You'll need to go to one of the parlors that handle that. So are we finished?"

The door opened and Lorelei walked in. "I gave the list to Williams to see if he can coordinate going after everyone. Most of the names were people from around the city. At least Louis provided some background on them. Should make it easy to track them."

"It's Saturday, most of them will be off work and home or out. Are you going to see how many you can nab today?"

"I'll see after Williams gets a plan ready for finding them. It will probably be this afternoon, so if you want to come, you're more than welcome."

Penny spoke. "I think I want to go back home to get my car and do a little shopping."

"Shopping? You already spent a fortune buying clothes up in Brinnon." I was surprised.

"I need jewelry. Earrings, necklaces, bracelets and/or broaches. I have to look glamorous coming from Vegas. I'm not the lovable country host I was in Michigan."

"Yeah, well, don't overdo it. You may lose all those country fans who watched your show religiously."

"I'll be discreet. Now if we have nothing else to do here, can we go?"

Lorelei laughed. "Nothing more to see here. We got what we wanted from Louis."

I stood and said, "I'll be back after I turn the glamour girl loose."

Bob Moats

We went out after saying our good-byes and I drove Penny back to the house.

"Have fun shopping," I said as I pulled up to the garage and opened it with the remote.

"You know I will," she said and kissed me. "Don't beat up any more suspects. You'll get a reputation."

I waited until she was safely in her car and then I drove out. It was almost eleven and I hadn't had breakfast. Not that I enjoyed breakfast, usually simple toast, nothing more. My stomach never woke until about two hours after I did. But now I was feeling hungry.

I pulled into a Burger King and got a breakfast sandwich at the drive through. I drove with one hand and ate with the other. Not smart, but I was trying to hurry back before I missed something.

I parked at the precinct lot and went in. Lorelei was in Lynn's old office and reading from a sheet.

"Is that the list of suspects?" I asked.

"Yep, Williams just finished it. Lots of big wigs on here. Studio people and professionals. Doctors, lawyers, financiers and all of them in the one percent."

"Maybe you should start with the doctors. They need to know if they have AIDS," I said.

"True. There are two on the list, both at LV Medical. Shall we go give them a thrill?" she said with a grin.

Network Murders

We went to her Mustang and I still had trouble getting in the thing. The door opening was too small and I was too big. Next time I would suggest taking my car. We drove out and arrived at LV Medical shortly afterward.

The receptionist smiled when Lorelei identified herself. She looked on her roster and said both doctors were in. I hoped we wouldn't have to wait forever for them but it turned out they both were on break. That was convenient.

An orderly guided us to the doctor's lounge and pointed us to the doctors. We went over and Lorelei held out her badge.

"Doctor Moor and Doctor Yellen, I presume?" she said with a smile.

They gave her the once over and acknowledged.

"May we sit and have a talk?" she asked then sat without waiting for them to agree. I pulled over a chair and sat next to her.

"Okay, I'm LVMPD homicide Lieutenant Paris and this Jim Richards, consultant. I need to know what you know about Percy Isham."

They both sat trying to look innocent. "Um, we've heard of him. What is this about?"

"And you are?"

"Doctor Steve Moor," he said.

"Well, Steve, were you two aware that the recently murdered Isham had the AIDS virus?"

"He was HIV positive?" Moor said, sounding shocked.

"Our coroner, when he finished the autopsy, reported that he had the virus. You both were seen attending Isham's home parties. Did you indulge in sexual relations with Isham or any of his guests?"

I liked that Lorelei would cut right to the heart of the matter. Both doctors sat and went quiet.

Yellen cleared his throat and said, "Yes, we attended his parties as guests, but we didn't participate in the debauchery. We just enjoyed watching."

"Peeping toms?" I said.

Yellen looked at me and said, "Voyeurs is more the term, thank you."

"So you went to his sex parties just to watch? How did you know Isham?" Lorelei asked.

"He was on the fund raising committee for the hospital. Actually he just joined to meet people. We got to know him that way. One night he asked us if we wanted to join in on a big party he was having. He never mentioned sex. We went to see what it was about. I wasn't into bi or gay sex, so we just watched. It was not something we wanted to participate in."

Network Murders

"Okay, now that you know about Isham and his AIDS, could you help us track a few others who may have participated?"

They looked at each other, and then Moor said, "It would be bad to have those people running around spreading the virus. What can we do?"

Lorelei put the list in front of Moor and said, "Do these names ring a bell?"

Both doctors looked at the list and nodded. Yellen said, "I know about a third of them. What can I do?"

"As doctors, you can help them. Call and tell them to get in and get checked."

Moor took out his note pad and wrote the names of those he knew. Yellen did the same.

"Now that you're going to take care of that, maybe you can give us an idea as to who would want to murder Isham?"

*

Chapter 19

Again they both agreed they knew little about Isham and why he was murdered.

"I'm sorry, I only knew Isham through the committee. He seemed very friendly. As to who would murder him, I don't know."

"Wouldn't you say that someone who found out that there was AIDS being spread at Isham's party might want to kill him for getting it?" I asked.

"Mr. Richards, anything is possible. Like you, we doctors don't work on conjecture, we need facts. I have no facts about this. So please excuse me if I have nothing to help you with. If I saw or heard something at the party or after, I would tell you," Moor said.

"After? What happened after?" Lorelei asked.

Moor hesitated. He looked at Yellen and then said, "As we were leaving we could see Isham was upset about something. He was talking to some rough looking individual and they seemed to be disagreeing about something. I don't think it was bad enough for murder, but Isham wasn't happy."

"Well, I guess that would be a fact. Thank you. Could you identify this rough looking character again?" Lorelei asked.

"I suppose we could," Yellen said.

Lorelei brought up the folder she had for the suspect list and opened it. From inside she pulled out a couple photos and spread them in front of the men.

"I pulled these photos out for dangerous suspects we have so far. Recognize anyone?" she asked.

They studied the photos and then they both pointed to one. Lorelei pulled the photo back and read the name written on the back.

Network Murders

She looked at me and said, "Gregg Sando."

I looked back to the doctors and said, "Did you notice any drug activity going on by the guests?"

I could see they were reluctant. I said, "No one is saying you participated, but we need to know if this man was bringing drugs to the party."

Moor finally spoke. "I didn't see who brought the drugs, but they were there. We don't use them. I've had to patch up too many victims of drug overdoses. I'm not fond of it."

Lorelei turned to me and said, "We need to find someone who saw Sando giving out the drugs before we can arrest him."

"Louis should know. He was everywhere," I said.

"I hate to go back to beat it out of him. Would you do it?" she said with a smile.

"It'd be my pleasure. Besides, it turns Penny on."

She turned back to the doctors and said, "Thanks for your candor. We may need you to give your statements about what you saw. Thanks," she said and stood. I followed her out of the lounge and back to the car.

I squeezed in and she drove out after calling Warren to take Louis back to interrogation.

"So far Louis saw Nate Bartan arguing with him over drugs. Now, according to the doctors, Sando is involved also. We're getting too many suspects," I said.

"And we are no closer to figuring out why he was murdered."

I thought for a moment then asked, "Were there any security cameras in or around the network building?"

"I had Warren check that out. He got nothing. Either the killer was clever and knew where the cameras were or he was lucky. CSI found nothing. The killer was in and out as far as they can tell. No trace left behind."

"Anything on the weapon?"

"Small caliber, no bullet striations in the system to identify the ownership. I was hoping it would match Bartan's gun, but it didn't. We still have diddle squat."

She pulled into the precinct and parked. We went in and found Warren standing outside one of the interrogation rooms.

"Did he complain about his living quarters?" Lorelei asked him.

"Constantly. I believe the holding cell guards wanted to shoot him."

"Thanks, we just have a couple questions then you can take him back. Maybe you can pretend he's escaping again and shoot him."

Warren laughed and said, "Don't tease me." He turned and went to his desk.

I looked into the room as Louis was pacing around. I guess they had decided not to handcuff him. Lorelei smiled and went in. I followed.

"Louis, we have a few questions to ask you. Sit down before you get hurt."

Louis glanced at me and sat. "What do you want now? Didn't I give you all the information before?"

"Well, there's one name you left off your list, Louis. Gregg Sando. Ring a bell?"

Louis sat back and tried to act unconcerned. But I could tell he was worried.

"Louis, you do know Sando, don't you?" I asked.

He was twitching his head around, looking at the room. He stopped then said, "I don't know any Sando."

"Louis, we have eye witnesses that Sando was at Isham's party. You mean you missed one guest even though you listed all those people?"

"Okay, maybe I didn't talk to everyone. There were a couple bad ass looking guys that I didn't want to get involved with."

Lorelei pulled the photo of Sando out again and set it in front of Louis. "Ring a bell now?"

He leaned in and looked. "Yeah, he was there. I didn't talk to him, I didn't like his looks."

"He's a wiseguy. Local numbers man and drug runner for one of the mobs. Know him now?"

"Like I said, I saw him but didn't associate with him. Did he kill Isham?"

"We don't know, Louis. But he's high on the list."

He got a strange little smile on his face then dropped it when he saw me watching him. I wondered what that was about. It wouldn't do much good to ask, he'd just lie.

"You never saw Isham and Sando talking or arguing?" Lorelei asked.

"Hey, I wasn't Isham's guardian. I didn't watch after him. I was busy watching the women."

"Louis, didn't you ever participate in the sex romps?" I asked.

"I wasn't invited and Isham told me to stay in the background. I would have loved to sock it to any one of those babes. But if I had, Isham would have thrown me out."

"And your fun watching would have been finished," I said.

"Yeah, something like that. I just did my job and let them have their fun."

"Your job was to fix broken things from the wild guests?" I asked.

"Yeah, just like that."

"Not much of a job," Lorelei said.

"Hey, he paid me well. I didn't complain."

"Okay, Louis, go back and rest for the night. We may need you in the morning."

"Oh man, can't I go home?" he whined.

"Not until we talk to a few more people. So relax and enjoy your stay." Lorelei stood and I followed her out. She called to an officer by the door and said to take Louis back to his cell.

We went to the office of the missing Lynn. I was missing her myself. Not that I didn't like Lorelei, but I was used to Lynn and Deacon.

"Are you chasing any more leads today? It is Saturday," I said.

"No. Go and enjoy the day. I'll probably wait until Monday before I chase any more ghosts. I may send a few officers out to pick up Sando and have him stay the weekend in lock up. Just think on his evil ways. I'll let you know what's happening."

"Thanks, I'm going home to watch Penny bury her jewelry in the back yard. She always was a pirate at heart." I left.

I called Penny to see what she was up to, but she didn't answer. That wasn't like her. I tried again and still no answer. Now I was worrying. I sped up a little to get there, avoiding the busy streets. I arrived and ran in to hear singing coming from Penny's bathroom.

I went to her door and listened. It was Penny singing along with a song by Adele. I think. At least it sounded like it. I carefully opened the door and Willy came flying out and attacked my leg. I reached down, picked him up and went in. Penny was in the shower with the curtain closed so she hadn't seen me yet.

I reached over and shut off the music from her little boombox on the sink. She suddenly stopped singing and didn't move. I knew she'd kill me if I scared her, so I said quietly, "Honey, I'm home."

She let out a scream that I hadn't heard since she found a spider in her oatmeal box. She reached out and grabbed a towel then pulled the curtain aside, glaring at me. I was ready to run. She had implements in the shower that would hurt. She suddenly calmed and said, "You're going to regret that." Then pulled the shower curtain back.

"Turn my music on again and get out. I'll deal with you later." The order came from the shower.

I turned the thing back on and made my escape, taking Willy with me. Misery loves company. I went to the living room and turned on the TV. I plopped on the couch and watched the news. Not that I cared for the news but I wanted to see if there was anything more about Isham and his AIDS. There was nothing. Shame, it would be left to us to alert all those people.

147

About twenty minutes later a fairly dry Penny came out in her fluffy bathrobe. She stood looking at me and said, "You could have called."

"I did, but you didn't answer. I guess your performance in the shower blocked out the phone's ring," I said.

"Okay, I'll give you that." She sat next to me and said, "So did you catch your killer yet or just rough up a few more people?"

"Which will make you frisky? I'll go for the roughing up."

"Good answer, follow me," she said and got up, heading to the bedroom. I wasn't going to complain.

*

Chapter 20

The phone rang around eleven and I debated on answering or just letting it ring. Penny said to answer it or she'd beat on me. I answered it.

"Hello?" I said, not able to see the caller ID. It was Lorelei. "What's up that you have to call me this late?"

Penny mumbled something about Lorelei missing me. I shoved her away. She was laughing under the covers.

"I sent men out to pick up Sando. Unfortunately he was murdered." I sat up on hearing that. "He was found in the alley behind the strip bar you went to. He was shot close range, one bullet to the head. Someone didn't want us to talk to him."

"The mob?" I asked.

"I don't think so. His men were enraged and blamed it on the police. We questioned them and they weren't aware of any hit on him by his own people. There's someone who wants to remain anonymous and is killing off people who could identify him. We need to talk. Sorry to call so late."

"It's okay. I'll be busy Monday with Penny's show premiere, getting her and everyone ready, so do you want to get together tomorrow?" I said.

"If you don't mind. You've done a bit of talking to the right people, including Sando. I want to get your take. Maybe you heard something that will shed light on this. Let's say we meet around ten?"

I thought about going to meet with Angelo to pick up his mom. "No, make it around noon. I have something to do in the morning."

"Sounds good. So we'll talk tomorrow," she said. Then she hung up and I put the phone back on the base.

I lay back and Penny popped her head out from under the covers. "Are you having an affair now? Should I worry?"

149

Network Murders

I looked at her and smiled. "You know full well I could never have an affair with a beautiful woman like Lorelei."

"Oh, and I'm not beautiful? Thank you," she said and went back under the covers.

I just sighed and said, "You know what I meant. Now go back to sleep. You need to look good for your show. Plenty of rest for you."

She didn't say anything. Then I could hear her soft snore. It amazed me how fast she could go to sleep. She'd never remember our conversation. I turned and tried to sleep. Visions of Sando with a bullet hole in his head ran through my brain. Was he in control of his situation? How did he lose it? What could he know that cost him his life? I rolled over and was asleep shortly after.

Penny was bouncing around the kitchen when I came out in the morning. She made breakfast and it was good. Eggs, bacon, toast and orange juice. I was amazed.

"So what's on your agenda today after we pick up Frances?" she asked me.

"Going to find out who killed our suspect last night. Don't you remember the phone call?"

She paused in her eating, thought for a moment then said, "Oh, yes, Lorelei's call. It used to be Lynn, now it's different. We need to see them again before the baby goes to college."

150

"They said they would be coming to your show Monday. Probably without the baby. But it will be good to see them. Okay, we have to meet Angelo. Are you ready?" I asked.

She finished the last bite of her food. "Ready to roll," she said and picked up Willy.

I pulled the mini-limo out from the garage and Penny got in. We drove to Angelo's apartment and he was standing outside with Sophia. He waved and came to the car. I opened the doors for them and they got in. We arrived at the private section of McCarran Airport and waited by the hangers where Gino's jet would park.

"So, Angelo, are you excited to see your mom?" I asked.

"Sure am, Mr. R, very excited. I'm happy that she can meet Sophia."

We talked a little more, then the jet came in. Angelo got out of the car and helped Sophia. Penny and I exited the car and we all went over to where the jet was being parked. The door opened and the flight attendant came down followed by Frances. She was looking fabulous and happy.

"Angelo!" she yelled.

"Mama!" he yelled back. They met halfway and hugged. Angelo introduced Sophia and she gave the young woman a hug.

Network Murders

Frances looked over to us and smiled. She motioned to us to come over. We went to her and she hugged Penny.

She laughed and said, "You brought the little dog." She ruffled Willy's head then turned back to Angelo. "You got my favorite room at the Tropicana?"

"Of course, only the best for you."

We all piled back into the limo and I drove them to the hotel. I pulled up to the front entrance to drop them off.

I stood by the car as Angelo was putting Frances' luggage on a cart. I said, "Frances, you have to get settled in and have a visit with Sophia and your son. Penny and I have to go chase criminals for a while but we'll be back later to visit."

"Thank you, Jim, for picking me up. I'll see you later," she said and hugged Penny again.

Penny and I got back in the limo and drove back to the house to switch cars.

"So it was good to see her again. Hopefully she can stay a little longer this week," I said.

"I hope so, too. Now are we going to the precinct?" she asked.

"Do you still feel like going?"

Bob Moats

"I don't have anything better to do, so I'll go to make sure Lorelei doesn't attack you." She kissed me on the cheek and got in the car.

We were on the road and arrived at the precinct shortly thereafter. Lorelei was talking to a couple of patrolmen when we entered the squad room.

"Jim, these are the officers who found Sando. I wanted to get their take on the crime scene. Hello, Penny. Did Jim drag you out here to listen to our boring work?"

"I don't mind. It gives me something to do before I go crazy waiting for tomorrow."

"I can imagine that would be stressful," Lorelei said.

"I'm not stressed, really, just anxious to start."

"Well, you're more than welcome to join us. Now we need to talk." Lorelei thanked the officers and they went off. She turned to the office and went in. We followed.

"Sit, relax. We have too much on our plate. So let's try and come up with some ideas or a plan to proceed."

We sat and Warren brought in a box of donuts. He handed them to Lorelei who opened the box and set them on the desk. "Thanks, Greg," she said to Warren, and he left.

"Now that we have nourishment, we can talk," she said with a grin and a big bite of a jelly filled donut. The grape oozed out and she caught it with her hand. Licking her fingers she said, "My weakness, nothing to do with

153

being a cop. I just love jelly donuts. Now do you have any ideas?"

"Backing up to the beginning, Isham was killed in his office. That sounds to me like all business. He could have been killed in his home, but that would be personal. This seems to be a hit. But with the death of Candy Cane in the same way, it now says that someone wanted people to shut up." I took a big bite of my donut, a cream filled that started to drip. I caught it and licked it up. "Now you tell me that Sando was murdered last night. But what did he have to do with Isham? Sando was mob, and he was harassing Isham over money owed. Sando may have found out who killed Isham. There was money involved, not where they could get to it, but Sando said Isham had a big stash of it somewhere." I took another bite.

"So you think this could be money related?" Lorelei asked.

"It's possible. If Isham had money stashed away, someone wanted it, including Sando. He acted like it was a lot of money. Or at least that was the impression he gave me. It would take a lot of money to justify murder. Maybe the killer thought Isham had the money in his office. Did CSI say that the place was searched?"

"They said it was a clean hit. In and out. So no searching the premises."

"Well, then maybe Isham led people to believe he had money stashed somewhere else. Maybe Isham confessed before he died that the money wasn't in his office."

"Candy had no interest in his money, did she?" Penny asked.

"When I talked to her she was more concerned over the cop, Nate Bartan, wanting to kill Isham. She never mentioned money," I said.

"Well, Bartan isn't talking, so he's not going to help."

"Speaking of Bartan, is he well enough to be interrogated?" I asked.

"I talked to him at the hospital. He was out most of the time but when he did come around, he said nothing. I mean nothing, not a word. I wasn't sure if his injuries disabled his speech, but he did ask the nurse for a new pillow. He's going to be uncooperative. IAB couldn't get much out of him either."

"Well, he went to visit Buzz with a gun and he attempted to shoot Warren. That says something," I said.

"Yes, it does. But it does no good if we can't get him to talk about why."

*

Chapter 21

"So far we know that Bartan was involved with Isham and not in a nice way. I'd move him up in the list of suspects," I said.

"Okay, but think on this. Being in the hospital, Bartan couldn't have killed Sando. Where does that figure in?"

"Now you're trying to confuse me." I laughed.

"Don't old people get confused easily?" she said with a smile.

"He's always confused," Penny said.

"But I'm not old and that's not nice to say. I have a young brain even if the body is slowing. Now let's get this finished up."

They stopped talking but gave me a smile.

"Okay, we really need to start talking to the party people, just to see what they have to say," I said.

Lorelei said, "I have to agree. I'm putting Warren and Williams on this to round up the suspects. We've talked to the doctors. I'm not liking them as suspects. They were creepy, but I don't figure them into this. There were about fifteen others on the list and I think we can talk to them in one setting. If we can gather them all together."

"I have a thought. Why don't we send out invitations to these people for a farewell party for Isham."

Lorelei just stared at me then said, "You think anyone will attend?"

"Can't hurt to try. Williams got all the phone numbers on his list. We can call and make it like we are good friends of Isham and say we are having a wake. I think we'll get a good number of people appearing," I said. "Get them in a group and let them start talking. There may be some good dirt to dish."

Lorelei smiled wide and said, "What the hell. It will save time and maybe someone will crack. Shall we invite the doctors?"

"Why not? They like to watch," I said and looked at Penny. "The good doctors are peeping toms, or so they say. I think they participated. Which is another good idea for the party. Someone will admit to having sex with the doctors. I think they lied anyway."

"Okay, shall we call a party planner or just go into this on our own?"

We spent the rest of the morning and part of the afternoon making plans and calling people. It was amazing that these so called friends of Isham didn't know about Isham's death. Which was good for us, they also didn't know about the AIDS. We didn't tell them about the AIDS, but they were surprised to hear Isham was dead. We arranged for a large room at a local restaurant just to keep it away from the condo.

"I guess the doctors didn't bother to call anyone to warn them about the virus. I want to call them, I have a good lie to tell them," I said.

Penny was playing with Willy on a desk in the squad room as we made party arrangements. She was looking bored but busy. I hoped it would take her mind off her show tomorrow.

Network Murders

I turned to Lorelei. "We need to bring Louis in on this. He's the one common denominator in this mess. Everyone knew him. If he's there, they may relax. We can make him the greeter at the door," I said with a laugh. "We can get him a blue greeter's vest like at Wal-Mart."

Penny shook her head and stood. "I need food," she said.

"I'm hungry also," Lorelei said.

"Well, I'll make it unanimous. I feel hungry too, so I guess we should call in for food."

"Call in, hell. I want a sit down meal. It's almost time for dinner," Penny said.

I stood, picking up my jacket from the back of the chair. "The boss commands, I obey. Lorelei, you may as well join us as I will be paying for this dinner."

The three of us went out to my car and drove over to a restaurant close by. It wasn't exactly Angelo's but it sufficed.

"So do you think this party will solve anything?" Penny asked as we waited for our food.

"It's more of an experiment, actually. We get everyone together, throw out facts about Isham and his AIDS, we may stir up a few people. I looked at the names and talked to half of these people. I'm sorry to say, but they are clueless. Clueless about life and where they are going. They want to party and leave reality behind. This news should shake them up and maybe catch a killer."

"Well, I wish you luck. So Tuesday night is party night in Vegas," Penny said.

"I got all but one acceptance. The reluctant person was a lawyer, of course. He probably suspects something," I said.

"I have Warren checking him out. I'm not fond of lawyers now since my ex, but we'll break him," Lorelei said.

I didn't want to laugh at Lorelei's situation, but I didn't like lawyers either. I thought about Alphonse Grisler and cringed. Grisler was now relaxing in a prison cell for his attempts at murder.

"Are you ready for tomorrow, Penny?" Lorelei asked her.

"As ready as I'll ever be. I need to go in earlier for a meeting with the network biggies then meet my new crew who will be doing the hard work. I've done this so long now, it's second nature. Put a guest in the hot seat and I move in for the kill." She grinned at the thought.

"Well, don't murder anyone on your first day, save it for the third or fourth show," I said.

Our food came and we ate with minimum talk. We were hungry. We finished and I paid, leaving a big tip. I had respect for wait staff and always supported them.

We went back to the precinct and continued our calls. After two hours of inviting guests for our sting, we had fourteen out of fifteen acceptances. I had called the doctors and explained that we would like to have them attend to help us find the killer. It involved them in the investigation and I figured since they were voyeurs, they would like that. It worked and they accepted. I just hoped everyone would attend. Even the killer.

"Okay, we have a party," Lorelei said. "Hopefully the guests don't find out about Isham's virus before they get there."

"I talked to the doctors about that. They apologized and said they were so busy that they didn't have time to call. I explained that it would be better if they didn't say anything until Tuesday night. They both had tests and said they didn't have the virus," I said.

"You believed them?" Penny asked.

"Since they say they didn't participate, no reason not to for now. We hopefully may get answers at the party," I replied.

"Well, this is a fine sting. Now can we go visit with Frances and see how she is doing?" Penny asked.

I said to Lorelei, "We've done all we can for now. Our next phase is the party. So I shall take my wife and go visit a mafia matriarch. We had better or we could sleep with the fishes," I joked.

"Where will you find fishes around here? We're in a desert," Lorelei said.

"I'm sure there are plenty of fish in Lake Mead. Anyway we need to go." I stood and Penny picked up Willy from the desk where he was sleeping.

"Take care, guys. Thanks for the help," Lorelei said.

We said our good-byes and left the station. We went back to the house to clean up. There is a smell in the police station that gets into your clothes and follows you. Penny and I took a shower together to save time. I didn't mind. We dressed in nice clothes to meet with Frances.

I got on the phone and called Angelo. "Is everything going well?" I asked.

"Real nice, Mr. R. Sophia and mom are getting along very well. It's all Italian around here, but we'll speak English when you get here."

I laughed and said, "Thanks, my friend. We are about ready to head out. Did you have anything planned for the evening?"

"No, we were just going to sit and talk."

"Well, ask everyone if they would like to go see a show," I said.

"Hold on," he said and I could hear him asking. There was some mumbling and he came back on. "What did you have in mind?"

"I can get us into the Cirque du Soleil show Love at the Mirage."

161

Network Murders

He went off again then came back. "Everyone is good with that. What time?"

"We'll pick you up in a half hour and the show will be starting at seven."

"Great Mr. R, we'll be ready," he said and we finished.

"Can you get us in the show?" Penny asked.

"Sure, I'll use your name," I said with a grin. "Actually I do know the manager of the show and they always have comp seats." I called my contact. Ten minutes later I had five tickets in Penny's name.

"You are terrible," she said.

"Well, it got us in the show didn't it?"

She went to finish dressing and we went to the limo again. I called ahead, told them to meet us at the front entrance, and we drove over. They were waiting for us as I drove up. The valet opened the door for them and they got in, Frances first, then Sophia.

"This is so exciting," Sophia said as she sat.

"Honey, when you know Mr. Richards, life is always exciting," Angelo said with a big grin.

*

Chapter 22

We arrived at the theatre and enjoyed the performance. Then we watched the fake volcano explode and flash in front of the building. I told everyone that Penny should go home to get some sleep for her show in the morning.

Angelo said, "Don't worry, Mr. R, I'll get Mom and Sophia to the studio in time for the show."

"Penny left word about all of you coming so you should have no problems getting in," I said.

Frances smiled and said, "If they give us a hard time I'll call Gino and have him take care of it." Everyone laughed.

She was quite a woman for a mob matriarch. She could even joke about it. I drove them back to the hotel and dropped off Frances, then took Angelo and Sophia to his place.

"See you in the morning," I said as we left them waving.

On the way back Penny was humming a Beatles tune from the show. She seemed happy.

"Excited?" I asked.

Network Murders

"Now I am. It will be fun to get back into network TV. Having all those many more people watching from all over the country. I eat it up," she said with an evil smile.

We arrived back home and I took Willy out for a walk. The strip in the distance was all lit up and looking beautiful. I heard the front door open and out came Penny.

"Don't you just love it out here?" she said.

"Yep, close enough, yet far enough. And we get our great view every night. Now you need to get some sleep."

I picked up Willy who was at my feet and led Penny back into the house. She went off to her bathroom to get ready for bed. I put Willy on his Bate's Motel chair and he curled up. I went into my bathroom and undressed, showered and went back into the bedroom. Penny was already in bed and sleeping peacefully. I liked that she could pass out so quickly.

I crawled in and turned on my side, looking at Willy sound asleep on his chair. I passed out myself shortly after. But not before I thought about the sting going on Tuesday night. I hoped everyone would attend and we'd catch our killer.

The next morning I got up, seeing Penny was gone from the bedroom. I went to her bathroom, the door was open and she was putting on her make up.

"Why are you bothering to put on makeup? In about an hour your makeup groupies will slap cold cream on your face to take it all off then make you look beautiful for the show," I said.

"I can't let anyone see me without makeup, even my makeup ladies."

"Penny, my love, they'll shake you like an etch-a-sketch and put a new face on you. But I understand, you have to look beautiful all the time." I left her to get some toast. I stood at the toaster and did a mental rundown of all the people who would be coming today. I hoped everything would go well.

Penny was ready, I was ready and Willy was in his travel bag. I decided to make Penny feel special so we drove in the limo. She was beaming as she watched the scenery go by.

I pulled into the studio lot and parked. We went in the employee's entrance and to her dressing room. Her girls were all ready for the day and welcomed her with a good luck banner above the dressing table. Penny hugged them all and sat for her makeover.

I wandered out to the studio where her show was going to be taped. The network came in over the weekend and redid the set. It looked much better.

I suddenly jumped when I heard a voice behind me. It was Gordy, Penny's producer.

"Well, is she ready? Mentally, I mean," he asked.

"As well as she'll ever be. How are you holding up?"

"I'm so nervous, I may pee my pants. But I'll make it through. The network biggies are all here in the conference room waiting to talk to Penny when she's done in makeup. God, I'll be glad when this first day is over."

"It will all be a memory soon. Are the guests here?"

"They both came in an hour ago to relax. The band is outside on the new stage getting ready. This is going to be a day to remember."

He got called by his assistant to come back to the conference room. Penny was ready to meet with the network people. Gordy excused himself and went off.

I sat in the first row of the seats for the audience and just relaxed. Nothing more I could do now. About ten minutes later the lobby doors opened and in came the audience. I stood and went up front to see if my people had arrived. I saw Angelo and his family. I waved and he saw me. I took them around the side and to the front where their seats were assigned.

"Just relax here. As you know from other shows you've attended it takes a while to get everything working." They settled in and I went to find more of my friends. I finally had herded in Lynn, Deacon, Trapper with Sam, Earl with Paula, Lacey with Mac and finally, Tracey alone. Everyone was seated and I introduced Frances to the others. I excused myself and went back to Penny's dressing room. She was getting the final touches and saw me.

"Sweetie, is everyone here?" she asked.

"Everyone but Buck and Maria so far. I'll watch for them."

The new stage manager came to her door with the sheets of info on her guests. She took them and read. I smiled at the man. "I'm Jim Richards, Penny's husband."

"Yes, sir, I know you. I'm Tim. Pleasure to meet you finally. I'm a fan of your books."

I thanked him and told Penny I was going to look for Buck. I went back out to the lobby and saw Buck coming up with Maria. I waved and led them to their seats. Buck remembered Frances from when we were in New York hunting for the missing niece of the Traviano mob family. He said his hellos to everyone and they sat.

The stage crew was getting the lights and props ready. It was a flurry of activity. It was now about ten minutes till taping and I got to see the guests in the back. Strange to see TV and film actors in real life. They looked different. Penny was asked to go to the side of the stage behind a curtain to wait for her entrance.

Tim, the stage manager, got on his mic and called for everyone's attention. The room of about two hundred people went silent.

"Thank you everyone for coming to this first taping of the new Penny Wickens Show. I'm Tim Barrows and I'm the director and stage manager. Please remain in your seats unless we say it's all right to move about. If you'll notice the sign above my head it prompts you to applaud. Only for the commercial breaks or to make the guests feel important." Everyone laughed. "This is the first taping of the new show and I'd like to bring out our host of honor, Penny Wickens."

Network Murders

Penny walked out to tremendous applause, everyone standing. I hoped Penny didn't cry and ruin her makeup. She waved and smiled, then Tim took her to her new easy chair where she would talk to her guests. He sat her and called up to the control room that they could take it from there shortly. They had the prompter ready for her to read from and she relaxed.

Tim went back out front and said to the audience, "Every host has a side person who helps with the show. I'd like to introduce Kent Harris, our new announcer." He motioned to a man standing beside a podium.

He was good looking, dressed in a suit and he said into his mic, "Thank you everyone. I'll be opening the show and then I'll turn it over to Penny. Then I'll be announcing the guests and the breaks. So just listen for the cues."

He had an announcer's voice, just right for the show. I didn't know about this and wondered if Penny knew she would be sharing the stage. I was sure that would be fine with her. I hoped.

They had all the overhead stage lights on and adjusted. The camera operators were moving the cameras into position and listening for their directions from the control room. Everyone was moving with the efficiency of having done shows like this many times before. Penny sat relaxing and looking comfortable. They had a fan off the side blowing at her to keep her cool in the hot lights.

Finally everything was ready. I had attended enough of Penny's show tapings to know what went on. I was getting nervous myself now. This was the big moment. They got Penny in position for her entrance.

Tim called for the taping and counted down. The monitors showed the credits rolling and images of Penny doing various things around Vegas. Kent Harris suddenly announced the show introduction from the prompter.

"It's the Penny Wickens Show! Today's guests are actress Patsy Harper and TV hunk Darius Curling from the show, 'LA Underground.' Let's give a big welcome back to the CW Network to our girl of the hour, Penny Wickens!"

The applause sign flashed but it wasn't needed. Everyone went wild and Penny was on camera, coming out from the back of the set and up to the chairs, this time carrying Willy. She stood smiling and waving as the crowd went crazy. I hoped again she wouldn't cry.

*

Chapter 23

Penny was holding Willy's paw and waving it, then the audience was signaled to calm down. Penny stood smiling and started.

"Thank you so much everyone. It seems strange that my show was just on last Friday, but now I'm going out to the nation instead of just Las Vegas. We're still here in Vegas and will be for all our shows. So many more celebrities and surprise guests to have at our disposal. For those of you who haven't seen me before, this is my dog Willy, named after one of our studio audience, Will Trapper. He's slouching down in his seat up front here." She pointed and one of the cameras cut to him. Everyone laughed as he covered his face. Then they cut back to Penny. "He's part of my wonderful husband's private investigating firm, Jim Richards Investigations and Security, right here in Las Vegas. Now that I've given a plug for my husband, I'd like to talk about our guests."

I grinned as I watched Trapper hiding his face with his hands. Penny went on about her guests and then sat.

"How are you today, Kent?" Penny asked her announcer. The camera cut to him.

"I'm doing real good, Penny. I'm so happy to be working with you on this venture." He was brief and knew his place was not to overdo his talk.

Back to Penny, she talked a bit about what she had been up to since her last network show. Then they went to a commercial break. Penny stood and handed Willy to one of her makeup ladies. They had taken care of the pup many times when Penny would bring him to the station.

She bopped over to me and gave me a big lip lock. I could feel her excitement. She turned and went to the front row where our friends were seated and greeted them. Trapper snarled at her and she laughed.

"You just had to do that?" he asked.

Bob Moats

"I just made you a famous person across the country. And what do you do? You cover your face. Shame on you."

Tim called for Penny to come back. She excused herself and went back up on the stage. The show continued with her first guest Patsy Harper, film actress of many well-known movies. They talked for the allotted time and then another commercial. Tim came up to her and was talking.

I found a stool, brought it up to the side and sat. The show was about half over and the TV star was up next. They came out of commercial and Penny introduced Darius Curling. The women all went crazy. He grinned and waved. Finally they settled down and Penny interviewed him.

Another commercial and then when Penny came back she talked about the final guest.

"We have something new for my viewers. On a new stage outside of the studio we have that great group from England, Twinkle, and they will be playing for us after this commercial."

Tim called for everyone to listen up. "Now, what we are going to do is take everyone out to the stage arena to watch the band play. Penny will talk from the bandstand and then the show will end. Everyone can get to their cars from the arena easily. I'd like to thank you all for being such a great audience and this show will be seen at eleven this morning, so you will all have plenty of time to go home and watch yourselves." They all laughed and Tim explained how to exit to the arena.

171

Network Murders

I pulled my friends aside and said, "We'll wait here for the mess to clear out then I'll take you to where you can see better."

The audience was outside standing in front of the band stand as the band tuned up. I took my friends to a platform on the side where they could see better. Tim called to the crowd and said for Penny to come out and introduce the band.

The camera pulled in close on Penny as she said, "Ladies and gentlemen, all the way from England, here's Twinkle."

She moved quickly off the stage as the band played a song. It was good and when they finished Penny interviewed the front man for a brief time, then they played another song as the show closed out.

Penny came off the stage as the band continued to play. She came up to me and asked, "Well, what did you think?"

"I think everything went well. Your big opening was great." Gordy came up and gave Penny a hug.

"Penny, the network execs were very happy with the show. They said you still had it," he gushed.

All our friends came off the platform and gathered around Penny, congratulating her.

The band was allowed to play two more numbers for the audience who stayed, which was most of them.

About forty minutes later the audience was gone and we stood by the side as the band tore down the equipment.

Three men in suits came up and the lead man said, "Penny, it was a great show. I'm happy we could get you back to our network. Now we need to get back to our headquarters to see about the ratings, but I'm sure they will be great." He turned and went off followed by the other two men.

"I'm glad they're done now. It's all downhill from here," Penny said.

I looked at our friends standing by and announced, "We are all going to Angelo's restaurant and have a celebration meal, on me."

That made everyone cheer and we left the studio.

Two hours later, after great food and conversation, our friends left. Penny and I sat with Angelo, Sophia and Frances at the table.

"That was fun and a great show, Penny," Frances said.

"Thank you, Frances. I'm so happy you could make it out. Thanks for being there."

"It was all so exciting, seeing the stars and the band. Just to watch a show being made was special. Thank you for having me along," Sophia said to Penny.

"I'm glad you and Angelo could come," she replied.

Network Murders

"Well, I don't know about you guys but I'm ready for a nap," I said.

"Yes, I could use one also," Penny added.

I stood and went to the front counter with the bill. I didn't want to pay it in front of Angelo. He would have made a fuss about my paying. I paid and came back to get Penny. I put a large tip on the table and said, "It's been fun. One night before you go back, Frances, we'll have all of you out to the house for a bar-b-que."

We said our good-byes and left. Willy was asleep on the front driver's seat and growled when I tried to move him over. "Hey, mutt. Don't growl at me unless you want to walk home."

Penny pulled him to her and snuggled his head. We arrived shortly after and let Willy do his thing.

We rested the night with beer, chips and TV, not talking. Penny was drooping and I told her to go to bed. I had a long day tomorrow with the party.

"Can I come?" she asked me.

I thought for a second and said, "I don't see why not. Just don't get into sex with anyone."

"Are you going to allow sex?"

I laughed and said, "I doubt there will be any sex once everyone hears about the AIDS. It's just an interrogation of suspects. But I think you should bring your gun."

"Jim, it's always with me. Even to the store."

"Well, don't shoot anyone for grabbing a dress that you want." I smiled and went to the bedroom.

*

Chapter 24

Tuesday morning, I went into the kitchen and told Penny I was going to see Lorelei.

"I'll probably see you later, after your show, and we can plot out our attack for tonight. You still want to come?"

"Of course. I wouldn't miss the fun."

"I'm glad you find it fun. I'll talk to you later." I kissed her and left. I made a detour to my office to see if Buck was awake and ready to help.

I went in the building and to his office. Mac was slaving over the paperwork.

"Hey, Mac, how's it going?" I asked.

"I can see why Buck is so much happier now. This is a pain to keep track of all these men."

"Is he in?" I asked.

"He's somewhere around the building. I heard him say something about an office of his own."

I laughed, went to the back, and looked in the store room. He was standing in the middle looking around the room.

"Got room for a desk?" I asked.

He laughed and said, "It ain't pretty but it will do. A few paneled walls to hide the shelves, it can work."

"Good, but think on it after we catch our killer. I have a lot to tell you about a little sting we are doing tonight. Follow me." I left the room and he followed. I went to my office and sat at my desk. He plopped down on the client chair and relaxed. I went through the plot Lorelei and I had hatched the other day.

"I love it, a going away party that will catch a killer. But what if none of these people did the killing?" he said.

"Well, we'll know then to look elsewhere. So you want to join the party?"

"I'll be delighted. Can I bust some heads?" he asked.

"Only if they get unruly. Then you are the bouncer," I said with a grin.

"It's a winner. What time?"

"We should be there by five to get ready. Lorelei is going to have her detectives around the room in case," I said.

"In case of what?"

"Anything unforeseen. We will just go with the flow and hope to flush out a bad guy, or girl."

"Think it could have been a woman?" he asked.

"Anything is possible. But honestly, I think the killings were committed by a pro. Maybe one of the guests hired someone to do the kills."

"I'm sure we can beat it out of a suspect or two. I haven't beaten up anyone in a long while."

"Hopefully we can get through the evening without beating anyone up. Now, how's Mac doing with your old job?" I asked.

"Good, better than I did. I'm not a paper pusher, I like the action. That's probably why I did so many fill-ins for missing guards. Just to get out in the field."

"You're going to be out in the field more now that you are one of the investigators. You'll get your hands dirty often."

"You mean like following unfaithful spouses?"

"Yeah, them too." I laughed and then picked up my desk phone. I called Lorelei to see how she was holding up. She came on after a couple rings.

"Hey, are you ready for tonight?" I asked. "I was coming to see you but stopped at my office first."

Network Murders

"Nothing much going on here. I had a long heart to heart talk with Louis and he's going to cooperate with us on this. I told him it would go well for him. He's getting a little stir crazy being locked up. I said if all goes well tonight he could go home."

"I'm sure that made him happy. He's neglecting his duties at the condos."

"I let him call his bosses, and he told them he was helping us find the killer of Isham. They were agreeable since they wanted it to go away. Is Penny doing her show today?"

"Yep, the show should be on in about an hour. I may watch it from here since there's nothing more to do until tonight," I said.

"Maybe I'll stop by just to get away from here. Weber is having a fit with half of our men out with flu. I don't want to end up writing tickets or directing traffic."

"Well, come on by. I'll hold a seat for you," I said.

She agreed and hung up. I sat back and looked at Buck. "This is a lonely business, mostly waiting for something to happen."

"I don't know about sitting for hours watching a cheating spouse," he said.

"It has to be done and we get paid for it. Now let's go out in the lobby and get ready for Penny's show." I stood and Buck followed me out to the front.

Lacey already had the big TV in the waiting area turned on and was relaxing on a couch.

"Good thing you're a good worker," I said. "Any other boss would fire you for sitting around."

"You'd never fire me. Who else would put up with you?" She gave me a big grin and turned back to the TV.

I wasn't going to disagree with her. She was a good worker and kept us going. I turned to see Mac come out followed by a couple guards who were in the building.

He smiled and said, "We wanted to watch Penny, too." I took the easy chair in the middle and everyone else grabbed the couches.

The front door opened and I looked over to see Penny come in. "Hey, babe, we are just getting ready to watch your show."

"That's nice. It was a good show today. Had Harrison Marlow on. He's even better looking in real life than in the movies. I was surprised to hear he's older than me. Then we had on Betsy Poplin the girl from the TV show, 'Sweethearts.' I think you would have liked meeting her. She asked me a lot of questions about you. Of course, I lied a lot."

"Of course, now she doesn't want to meet me," I said.

"Nope, she has a new view of you."

Network Murders

"Thank you for disparaging my image," I said as she came over and stood above me.

"Are you going to be a gentleman and offer me your seat?"

"Nope, I'm not a gentleman according to Betsy Poplin's new opinion," I said with a smirk.

She sat on my lap, hard. "Okay, I'll just rest here then."

I didn't move, she didn't move, so we just sat there. Lacey turned the channel to Penny's station and we watched the morning show with five people all trying to be funny about things going on in the world. I hoped this show wouldn't prevent people from watching Penny's show. Maybe Isham wasn't all that good at programming schedules. That was no reason to murder him though.

The office phone rang and Lacey jumped up to answer it. She called to me and said someone wanted to talk to me. I pushed Penny up and slid around her. She plopped back down on the chair. I knew I'd never get it back now.

I went to take the phone from Lacey and said hello.

"Mr. Richards?" came a female voice. I said yes. "I need to talk to you about Candy Cane. Where can we meet?"

"Why don't you come to my office?"

"I don't want to be seen going in there. How about we meet at Little John's Pub on Gass by Third Street? Say, in an hour?"

I looked over to the TV and said, "Make it an hour and a half and I can."

"I'll be there," she said.

"How will I find you and who are you?" I asked, but she hung up. I didn't like this. I just had the tingle again. My tingle was usually ninety percent right when something was wrong. I went back and stood behind Penny relaxing in the chair. She looked up at me.

"Anything important?" she asked.

"Might be, won't know until I go check it out." I was interrupted by the front door opening, and in walked Lorelei.

Penny smiled and said, "Good, we have a party now."

Lorelei came over to us. "Did I miss anything on your show?" she asked Penny.

"Nope, just starting. Have a seat."

I stopped Lorelei and asked, "Do you have to be back at the precinct anytime soon?"

She said, "No. Why?"

Network Murders

"I have to go see a woman about Candy Cane and I may need back up. I may take Buck with us also. I'll explain after the show."

She agreed and then went around to the couch and sat. Penny's show came on and we watched. It was a good show like Penny said and then it ended. I called Buck to follow me and asked Lorelei to join us. She did, followed closely by Penny. I didn't want to tell Penny to go away so I let her follow.

I went into my office and the women took the chairs while Buck stood behind them.

"I got a call about an hour ago from some woman who wanted to talk to me about the late Candy Cane. She didn't identify herself and wouldn't come here. Said she didn't want to be seen here. She wants to meet me at a bar in the downtown area by Fremont Street."

"Sounds like a set-up," Buck said.

"I think so too. So if you and Lorelei could go in the bar before me and watch my back, it would be helpful."

They both agreed. I looked at Penny and said, "I think you should stay here. It may be too dangerous."

"If you are going to get killed in a set-up, then I'll go out and buy a nice black outfit for your funeral," she said with a grin.

*

Chapter 25

We left my office and went back to the lobby. Everyone was still sitting around talking about the show.

"Are we going to get any work done today?" I asked. Mac and the guards went back to their office, Tracey went back to the front and Lacey went back to her desk. "Good show, Penny," she said as she went by us.

"Thanks, Lacey. While the private investigators and the cop go out and get shot, I'm going shopping. Hold my calls," she said with a smile, kissed me and left with Willy who had been sleeping on the counter.

"Your wife is a funny person," Lorelei said.

"You should see her in bed. Well, maybe not, too personal. Shall we go to our set-up?" I said.

We went out to my car and drove up the boulevard to just before Fremont, then I turned left on Gass and drove to the bar.

"You two go in and I'll wait a couple minutes before I go in and see if I can find this mystery woman. I don't have to tell you how to watch my back. Please do, I didn't wear my bullet proof vest today."

Lorelei and Buck got out and went to the front door. Buck looked back to me in the car and grinned. I'm sure he was thinking about Lorelei's posterior as she moved ahead of him. She did have a nice caboose. I waited for them to get settled and then I exited the car. The place was not much of a bar. It was just a small building that looked like it was built when Las Vegas was being formed. It probably was a local watering hole for the people who lived close by. The tourists would never come here for a drink.

I entered and waited a moment for my eyes to adjust to the dim lighting. I hated that. It would give time for someone to attack and I wouldn't see them coming. I could finally see the place and it looked as old as the outside. Reminded me of a western saloon, complete with a foot rail at the long bar. There were eight people sitting in various places around the room.

I looked around and saw a woman sitting by herself at a table. I presumed it was her. Buck and Lorelei must have figured it was her also as they were at a table nearby. I went to her and asked, "You the friend of Candy Cane?"

She looked up at me and said, "Richards?"

"That's me. And you are?"

"Sally, that's all you need to know. Sit. Let's talk."

She had the chair with her back to the wall. I had to sit with my back to the room. I wasn't fond of sitting that way. Too many ways to be jumped. But I felt safe knowing Lorelei and Buck were watching from a nearby table. I sat.

"Okay, you set up this meeting. What do you want?"

She looked around the room and then leaned in to talk quietly. "I was a friend of Candy. She would tell me everything she had in her little head. She told me some interesting things about a party she had attended. Do you know about it?"

"I do. What did she tell you?"

"You tell me what you know and I'll tell you if you need to know what she said."

I didn't like this runaround. Was she pumping me for information to see if I knew much about the case? Maybe she was going to see if I knew too much and then have me taken out.

"I'm investigating the situation and that's about all I can tell you. If you have something, tell me or I'll walk out of here." I waited to see what she would do.

Sally sat quietly then said, "Candy was afraid of someone. From what I got from her, I think it was a cop who found out she possibly knew where Isham had hidden a small fortune in cash. Isham was pretty lucky at his gambling and would stash the winnings. Candy wasn't really sure where he kept the money, but she worried that the wrong people thought she did. When I heard she was murdered, I figured someone thought she did."

"Candy told me about the cop, and he's resting in the hospital right now from a gunshot by a cop. He's not talking, but it will only be a matter of time before he does. I've heard about this money from a local hood named Sando. Ever heard of him?"

"Sando, sure. He's bad news, should be put away for the crimes he's done."

"He was put away. Bullet to the head. You didn't hear about it?"

She looked surprised. She thought a moment then said, "No, I hadn't. Well, it's for the better. He was rotten and a waste of life. He didn't know where the money was?"

"If he did, he didn't tell me," I said.

"Candy said she thought Isham had it hidden at his condo. But she was killed before she could do anything to find it."

"Isham's condo is being investigated by the police. She wouldn't be able to get in."

"She had a key. Isham gave it to her to help with his orgies. Did she have a key on her after she was killed?"

"I don't know. I'll have to ask the cop in charge. You think Candy may have been killed for the key?"

"I have my suspicions," she said, looking around. Probably for someone listening. Of course Buck and Lorelei were close enough to hear us. She gave them the eye.

I turned to Lorelei and said, "Excuse me, Lieutenant Paris, were any keys found on Candy Cane the day she died?"

Bob Moats

Lorelei smiled and said, "There were no keys found on the body when we investigated the murder."

Sally about had a fit. "You brought the cops! I didn't say to bring any cops!"

"Sorry, but I never leave home without one. This is Lieutenant Lorelei Paris, the investigating officer on Isham's murder. And now Candy's. She'll just sit and observe."

Sally looked like she wanted to leave. "Relax, Sally. She's not here to arrest you. Or should she?"

"I didn't do nothing! I just wanted to tell you about what Candy knew. I'm trying to help and you bring the cops."

"Sally, we're trying to solve a murder. If you know something, you need to help us."

"All I know is poor Candy may have known about the money. It's my opinion that's what got her killed. That's all."

"Well, it's a big help. Now if we could find out who wanted to know about that money, we might find the killer."

"I don't know nothing else. Honestly," she said, eyeing Lorelei.

"Again, it's something. Every little bit of information leads us to the killer. Thank you so much for your time." I stood and was ready to leave when she stopped me.

187

Network Murders

"Don't informants get some kind of pay for their information?" she said.

I could now see her motive. I dug into my pocket and came up with a fifty. I handed it to her and said, "Yes, I should have rewarded you. Thank you. Now if you hear anything else, call me. You know the number."

I signaled to my friends and they followed me out. In the sunshine I had to let my eyes adjust again. We stood outside the bar and Buck said, "I wanted to bust some heads."

"Next time, Buck. We don't always get the good situations. So what did you think?" I asked Lorelei.

"I'm sure she was sincere, but I think she was taking advantage of the situation to make a little cash," she said

"Well, she knew about the stash of money. That was mentioned a couple of times. Maybe there's something to it, that the money had to do with his death and not the AIDS. If Isham did have the money hidden in his condo, maybe you need to have a crew find it."

"I'll talk to CSI and have some of my men go help to tear the place apart. Can't hurt."

"Well, we still have our little orgy tonight to work the other angle, the AIDS," I said. We all headed to my car. "Buck, you may still get a chance to bust some heads tonight."

He grinned and got in the car. We drove back to the office and Lorelei said she was going back to the precinct to get her people ready for tonight. She left.

Buck and I went in the front door and I said hello to Tracey. We entered the inner lobby and Lacey was at her desk working on some paperwork. I hoped it was the reports she always complained about.

"I'll need your report on this case, don't forget. I'd hate to have to track you down," she said to me as we went past the counter. I just waved and went into the back. Buck said he was going to check on Mac and split off from me.

I entered my office and found Penny at my desk. She smiled at me and said, "You lived. Darn, and I wasted lots of money on a black dress. I'll have to save it for later."

"Yep, I'll bury you in it," I joked.

"Don't worry, I'll out live you. You're on a collision course to death," she said.

"Now that isn't nice. I plan on living a long time."

"Okay, I'll let you," she said with a smirk.

*

Chapter 26

"Fine, now get out of my chair so I can look official," I said and prodded her to move.

"Okay, okay. You aren't very nice today."

"I'm nice every day, just not when you're around," I said.

She stood and gave me a kiss. "Then I should stay away from you so you'll maintain your nice persona."

"Works for me. When are you going to start?"

She kissed me again and walked out of the room. I watched her leave. She still had a great body that still turned me on. I may be a senior citizen, but I'm not dead yet.

I sat in my chair and reached for the desk phone. I called Lorelei and waited for her to answer.

"Hey, Jim, did you miss me already?"

"How's your team holding up? Are they ready for the orgy?"

"I warned them that if any of them start to undress they'll be back in school safety as crossing guards. I talked to CSI, and they are going to give the condo a good going over. I said I could send a couple men to help but they said they could handle it. We're still a little light on men here."

"Hopefully the ones with the flu have only the one day flu," I said.

"We've gotten back a few men and women, so I'm not going to be issuing tickets anytime soon. I think we should meet at the restaurant by five to get ready. That will give us an hour to prepare."

"Works for me. I'll see how many people I have who can help. Can I bring a few security guards to handle the crowd?"

"That may be a good idea. They can guard the doors in case anyone tries to skate out."

"I'll talk to Buck. Well, I guess we'll see you at five. Talk later," I said and hung up.

I left my office and went to find Buck. In his office Mac sat with a couple of the guards.

"Where's Buck, Mac?"

"He went back to play in his new office," he said with a grin.

I turned and went to the store room. Buck was sitting on a chair in the middle of the room looking around. I tried not to laugh.

"Hey, buddy, I need to talk to you."

"Shoot, I'm listening."

"We'll need a few guards for the orgy tonight. Can you arrange that?"

"Of course. I am still in charge even if Mac is running the business. How many men?"

"Let say four. To watch the doors in case anyone tries to leave before we talk to everyone."

"You got it. I'll go talk to Mac," he said and stood. He went out of the room and I was alone. I looked around and decided the room, with a little fixing up, would be big enough for Buck. I figured I'd hire a couple carpenters to work on it that week.

I left the room and went out to the lobby. Penny was sitting with Lacey at her desk. Willy was on Penny's lap sleeping. I swear that dog does nothing but sleep. I wish I could.

"Hey, sweetie, had enough of looking official?" she said.

"Nope, I need more power," I said with a grin.

"You need to show up more often to look like you own the place," Lacey said.

"If I'm here then I'm not working. If I'm not working we don't make money and I can't pay you."

"Okay, fine with me, stay away," Lacey said with a smirk.

"Well, you're still the boss," Penny said as she woke Willy and stood. She kissed me and said, "I'm going home to be domestic. The house is getting a little messy. Don't forget to pick me up for the orgy." She went around the counter and out the front door.

"Going to orgies now? Is your love life starting to suffer?" Lacey asked.

"No, it's business. Part of the Isham murder case. No orgy, just fact finding. Now if anyone needs me, I'll be in my office pouting." I turned and went through the glass door towards my office.

Buck stopped by to tell me he had the guards.

"Have them meet us there at five. You can lead the attack."

"Will do. See you then." He went off and I sat back in my chair, staring at Penny's poster of her in a bikini. We were heading into winter in Vegas so she was not swimming in the pool as often. Even if it was heated. Vegas wasn't cold enough in the winter to prevent swimming, but Penny was funny about swimming in the winter. It was more mental than reasonable. I just daydreamed until three o'clock then went home.

Penny and I were ready just before five and I got the car out, then we drove to the restaurant and parked. I didn't see any cop cars so I figured they didn't want to scare anyone off. We went in and found Lorelei talking to her men. Behind her was Buck with his men.

Network Murders

Lorelei came over to us. "Jim, everything is going smoothly. I've got Louis sitting in the banquet room and I'll have him at the door when the people start to arrive. I have Warren with the guest list to check them off as they arrive. We can start once they all are in the room."

Buck came over and said, "I got my men ready to go. I have them in civvies. Otherwise their uniforms might frighten someone."

"Good thinking, Buck. Post them by the doors, the front and the one to the kitchen. I see an emergency exit, so put one man there too," I said.

He went off to get them ready.

"Williams will make sure no one goes back out once they are in. He has a couple men to help. We shouldn't have any problems," Lorelei said.

We walked around the room to get the lay of the land. Then we went to Louis and got him ready.

"That's all I have to do? I identify the people coming in and let your man know?"

"Yes, Louis, that's all you have to do. You cooperate and then we'll let you go home," Lorelei said.

He looked happy at that, and she took him to the banquet room door where Williams was standing with his clipboard.

Penny turned to me and said, "I'm going to sit at the bar and relax. This should be fun." She gave me a peck on the cheek, went to the back of the room and sat at the small bar. We decided to serve liquor to get the crowd loosened up and talking.

Just before six, a couple guests started to arrive. Louis went into his act and greeted them. They knew Louis by sight from Isham's condo, so they relaxed. Warren checked them off on his list and told them to go find a seat and wait for the wake to begin. I wondered if Isham would have enjoyed his own wake.

Forty minutes later we had all but three guests registered. One of the missing people was Doctor Yellen. Doctor Moor came earlier with an attractive woman who was not on the list but we let her enter.

"I'll give the last three people fifteen minutes, then we'll start. Some of these people are getting restless," Lorelei said.

"Let me try something," I said and went to the front where we had a small platform set up with a microphone. I stepped up to the platform and turned on the mic.

"Good evening everyone. I'm Jim and I'm glad you all could come here tonight to honor Percy Isham who was taken from this world too early. I ask you to be patient while we wait for a couple more people to arrive. If they aren't here in ten minutes, we'll start."

One man in the group called out, "When's the fun begin?"

A woman yelled to him, "Arthur, you wouldn't know fun if it grabbed you by the ass."

Network Murders

The group laughed and the man yelled back, "Why don't you drop your clothes and I'll show you some fun, Sue?"

"Don't flatter yourself, Art," another woman yelled. "I've seen the fun you say you can provide. It's not much."

Art went quiet as the group laughed harder.

"Okay, everyone, please calm down. We need to get serious to start. Then you can have all the fun you want." I said into the mic. "I'll go check to see if we can start."

I left the podium and went to Lorelei who was standing by the entrance. "Have our missing guests shown up yet?"

"All but Yellen. I wonder if he's avoiding us because he's guilty. I'll have an officer go see if he can be brought in for questioning."

"Good idea. Shall we start?" I asked Lorelei.

"May as well see what we can get accomplished. Let's roll."

We went to the platform and I called for attention. Everyone went quiet and I said, "You have all been invited here because of your participation in the orgies that Isham held in his condo. We have some information to tell you and we also need to question each of you. This woman standing next to me is Homicide Detective Paris, and she, along with her men, will be talking to each of you. You can still relax and visit the bar, but no one will be leaving until you have been talked to."

"What the hell, you got us here to interrogate us?" one man yelled.

"Yes, and give Percy Isham a sendoff into the great unknown. This is a murder investigation, in case you haven't heard. Percy Isham was murdered and all of you are now suspects."

*

Chapter 27

"Suspects? What do you mean suspects?" a man yelled from the back of the group. "Why would we want Percy to be murdered? Hell, he threw great parties. What would be our motive?"

I figured he was the one lawyer listed in the group. "Well, there is one big motive." I looked at Lorelei. She nodded. "You, sir," I said to the lawyer, "would you say that if someone found out that they were deliberately being exposed to AIDS, would that be a good motive for someone to kill the person spreading the virus?"

The man thought, then said, "I suppose that would be a motive and it has been in the past. I remember a case last year that…" He paused and then looked shocked. "Hey, are you saying that Isham had AIDS?"

I hoped the cops and Buck's men could contain the group if this went crazy. "It was reported by the coroner that Isham did have the virus. We suspect he may or may not have known he had the virus. But we have to know if it could be a reason to kill him."

Everyone began yelling and talking. It was not getting out of hand but they definitely didn't like the news.

"Do we have it?" one woman asked.

"I can't answer that. I don't know. You'll have to see a doctor to be checked," I said.

One woman stood, looking pale, and headed for the door. Two of the officers blocked her, turning her back to her chair. The group was still upset, but thankfully they didn't cause trouble.

One man stood and asked, "You think one of us found out and killed Isham in retaliation?"

"We suspect it's possible, but we need to talk to everyone to eliminate suspects. We need to know where each of you was during the time Isham was murdered. So if you have an alibi, it better be verifiable. Now Detective Paris and her detectives will be talking to each of you individually. So please be comfortable until you are called. Oh, and unofficially, the bar is open."

Lorelei stepped up to the microphone and said, "We'll be calling to each of you to talk, so be patient as Mr. Richards said." She signaled to Warren and Williams to join her. She stepped off the platform and the three of them divided the room into three groups of five people each.

Lorelei came to me and asked, "Would you sit in with Williams to help? He's a decent detective, but he's not great at questioning."

"Sure, I've known Williams for a while now and I understand," I said. I went over to him and we selected five people to question. We took them to one corner of the room and then asked a woman to follow us to another table. We sat and Williams began.

"Now, what is your name?" he asked.

"Linda Harden," she responded.

Williams ran through his copy of the guest list and checked off her name. "Now where were you last Wednesday at nine in the evening?"

The woman thought a moment then said, "I was at a dinner party with friends."

"They can verify you were with them all evening?" Williams asked.

"I certainly hope so. They're good friends and will back me up."

Williams pushed a pad of paper to her and asked her to write the names of a few of those friends. She took out a small phonebook from her purse and wrote names and numbers on the pad. She finished and pushed the pad back.

"May I ask how well and how long have you known Percy?" I asked.

"About a year. We met through friends at one of his parties. He was a delightful, funny man. Everyone liked him, including me. I would never murder him," she replied.

"Evidently one person didn't like him," Williams said. "Thank you, Linda, we'll be checking your alibi."

"I never had sex with him. Do you think I have the virus?" she asked.

"We can't say, but it would be best to get checked," I said.

She nodded her head, looking distressed. Williams told her he was finished with her and she went back to the group. He stood and went to get the next person.

We interviewed all five of our suspects and none jumped out as being a possible killer. I stood and went over to Buck who was sitting with Warren as they questioned their people. He looked up at me and whispered, "None of these people look good to me for the murder."

I leaned down and said, "Same here. I'm going to check with Lorelei." I left him and went to the table where Lorelei sat alone.

"I don't suppose you got a hit?" I asked.

"They all had alibis, but we'll need to check them out. How was your group?"

"Same. I think this is going nowhere. Maybe this is the wrong direction, and the money angle was right. Have you heard from CSI on the condo search?"

"I'll call them. They should be finished by now." She stood and took out her cell phone but before she could call, it rang. She answered.

"Detective Paris," she said. She listened for a moment and then hung up.

"Timing. That was the CSI shift leader. He said they found a safe in the bedroom closet behind a hidden panel. It was opened and empty. The killer got to it. They said there was no forced entry, so I'm thinking it was Candy's killer using the key she had."

"I'm sure they are checking for prints."

"They said they got a partial from the safe and will run it. He'll let me know when and if they get a match."

"Well, we're finished here. What do we do with all these people now?" I asked.

She smiled and said, "The room is rented until eleven. Let them have it to their own devices." She went to the platform mic again and said, "Everyone, thank you for your help. We have some checking to do, but you are all free to go. Just don't leave the city. This room is open until eleven. The bar is also open so you can stay to talk or whatever you want. Just don't destroy the room."

She left the platform, went to the front door and said to Louis, "You can go too, Louis. Thank you for your help. We may need you to answer a few more questions as they come up, so stay handy. I'll have an officer drive you home." He smiled and quickly left the room. She told one cop to take him home, and he went out.

I looked around the room. People were talking quietly to each other. It wasn't much of a party mood.

Penny came up to me and said, "Well, that was interesting. Not as exciting as I hoped it would be."

"How exciting did you want it?" I asked.

"I thought maybe someone would confess and hold the room hostage with a gun. I wanted to shoot someone." She gave me her evil grin.

"I really regret getting you that gun sometimes. But for as many people that you have shot and saved the day, I guess it was worth it," I said.

"You betcha. Now can we go?" she asked.

I looked at Lorelei, and she said, "I got nothing more. Now I have to justify this expense of the evening to Weber. I hope we get something out of this." She turned and went out of the banquet room.

I took one more look at the people. They weren't in a party mood. But I was sure that drinks would flow. It was good that it was a cash bar. I felt sure Weber would have been pissed if the LVMPD had to pay for it.

"Okay, let's get out of here. Let me talk to Buck first and I'll meet you at the entrance." She kissed my cheek and went out. I headed to where Buck stood talking to his guards.

He turned to me. "Well, that wasn't very exciting."

"Same thing Penny said. I had hoped we'd get something out of this. I'm going to take Penny home and I'll see you in the morning." I thanked the guards and went out to where Penny was standing at the front door.

"Some man just tried to proposition me. I almost took him up on it, but he wouldn't go for a grand."

"A thousand dollars for you? I'd turn it down too." I grinned and took her out the door as she was hitting my arm.

We went to the car and drove out.

"Are you hungry?" I asked.

"Actually, I am. Shall we go to Angelo's?"

"You read my mind. We need to find out how he's doing with Sophia," I said and steered the car in the direction of Mama Mia's.

We went into the restaurant and Angelo was not at the front door like he usually was. We found him at a table with Sophia and his mother.

"Mr. R, good to see you and the Mrs. Come sit," he said and stood.

We said our hellos to Sophia. Penny went to give Frances a hug and we sat.

"Did you catch your killer yet?" Frances asked.

"Nope, we're still looking though. It's not a fast process like on TV. In real life it takes longer than an hour," I said.

Frances laughed and said, "The movies and TV even make mob family life look more dangerous than it is. I get bored most of the time. Not like in the old days where made men feared they'd be whacked anytime. I always worried about my Angelo. I'm glad he's out of the family business."

"I am too, Mama," Angelo said with a smile. "I am too."

*

Chapter 28

A perfect meal prepared by my daughter, Carol. She came out to say hello and talked a bit before Angelo chased her back into the kitchen. Penny and I were wearing down and said we were leaving. I left a big tip since Angelo insisted on paying for our food. We said our good-byes to Sophia and Frances.

We went back to the car and arrived home shortly after. Willy was bouncing around when we came in, so I went to feed him as Penny went to the bedroom. I got a couple beers and chips and went to the bedroom. Penny had the TV on and was resting in bed sitting up. I handed her a beer and she thanked me.

"So what are you going to do now?" she asked.

"Sleep, I hope," I replied.

"No, sweetie, about the case. Did you get enough from the people tonight to decide what you're going to do?"

"Well, we have another avenue of thought. Seems Isham had a stash of cash. I like that, stash of cash. Anyway, his condo was searched and they found a wall safe that was empty. We had information that Isham had a lot of money hidden away. We think he may have been murdered for the money. It's getting complicated now. But we'll sort it out."

"I hope so. It would be nice to solve the case on your own, without Lynn and Deacon."

"Don't forget Lorelei is helping. It's her case actually. At least from the police side. I hope I do solve it so I can get paid. Although the network put a big retainer on it already."

"I have faith that you'll catch the killer." She kissed me and sat back to drink the beer and watch TV.

I was too worn out to watch TV or drink beer. I told Penny I was going to sleep and turned on my side.

Network Murders

I must have gone out fast, because the next thing I knew, Penny was waking me in the morning. "What? I want to sleep in," I mumbled.

"I'd let you, but you have a phone call."

"I didn't hear my cell phone buzz," I said.

"No, it's the house phone. It's Lorelei. She said she called your cell phone but got no answer."

I reached over to the bed stand and picked up my cell phone. It was shut off. "Damn, I keep doing that in my sleep."

I got up and went to the phone extension in my home office. "Hey, Lorelei, sorry I didn't catch you on my cell. What's up?"

"CSI got a match on the partial print from Isham's safe. It's from a hit man named Tommy Spadero, nasty guy according to his rap sheet."

"Well, that would explain the professional hits on Isham and Candy. Maybe even Sando. Any idea where to find him?"

"We got a BOLO out for him, but if he already grabbed the money he could be long gone. We at least have an idea on who is behind this now. What do you have planned for today?"

"Well, I was going to see what you came up with on the alibis. Are you working on that?"

"I got Williams and Warren on it. So far more than half of the suspects are no longer suspects," she said. "We haven't found Yellen yet. He was supposed to work at the hospital this morning but never showed. I talked to Moor, and he said he had no idea where Yellen is. Feel like taking a ride?"

"I guess so. Where to?" I asked.

"Yellen has a cottage out on Lake Mead. I thought I would get out of town and wanted company."

"Sounds good to me. I'll meet you at the station in a half hour. How's that?"

"Works for me, see you then." She hung up and I stood looking out the back window to the pool. I'd be glad when summer came back so Penny would be swimming again before going to work.

I dressed and went out to the kitchen. Penny was working on eating her oatmeal. I kissed her and said, "I have to go, taking a scenic ride out to Lake Mead. We may find our missing suspect and hopefully the killer. That is, if Yellen is working with the hit man."

"Hit man? You found a hit man?" she asked.

"Long story, I'll fill you in later." I ruffled Willy's head, kissed Penny and left the kitchen, going to my car.

I arrived at the precinct, went into the squad room and found Lorelei talking to Warren. I went over to them.

"I think you need back up," Warren was saying to her.

"I'll be alright. Just check on the rest of the alibis." She looked at me and smiled. "Ready to go?"

"Me and my Glock are ready. Do we need back up?" I said to Warren.

"She wants to go see this missing doctor who's possibly the connection to the murder and she doesn't want back up to follow," he said.

"Don't worry, I'll be there," I said. "We'll be careful."

"You get in any trouble, call," Warren said and went off.

"Let's get moving," Lorelei said to me.

We got into her Mustang, much to my dismay. I squeezed in and buckled up. She drove out and headed towards Lake Mead.

A while later we arrived and she drove to an address that she had checked with Google maps before I got to the station. It was a nice cabin on the lake, well-kept and clean looking. Yellen must have had a caretaker. Lorelei parked and we went to the door.

She knocked and waited. No answer. She tried again, still no answer. I was snooping around the front windows and saw nothing.

Bob Moats

"I'm going around the other side," I said. She nodded and went the other way around the building. I got to the patio doors in the back facing the lake and looked in. I yelled for Lorelei when I saw Yellen on the floor. She came running around and up to me.

I had my Glock out, and Lorelei tried the patio door. It wasn't locked. We entered carefully. I was watching for anyone in the building while Lorelei went to check Yellen. She looked up to me and said, "He's dead."

We both went through the house checking for others. We found no one.

"I need to call the local sheriff and report this." She pulled her cell and placed the call. Then she called Warren and told him to get a team of forensic techs there to examine the place. We waited for the local cops to show.

I went out back and stood looking at the lake. Lorelei came up and stood next to me.

"Okay, Yellen must have known about the money. He didn't want to get his hands dirty so he hired Spadero to find out where the money was. It looks like Spadero may have double crossed Yellen," she said.

"I'm thinking that also. There must have been a lot of money in that safe to go through all this."

"I had Warren pull Yellen's financials this morning. He was just about broke. Isham's money would have been a big help for him. I talked to Moor when I called to see if Yellen got in to work. He said Yellen had a gambling problem. He tried to help Yellen but he was told all was

209

good. Moor said he thinks Yellen used local bookies to place bets. Maybe they didn't like him not paying his debts."

"I thought about that. My feeling is that bookies wouldn't kill because then they couldn't collect. I think Spadero got greedy and wanted the money for himself. He shot Yellen and made off with the cash."

We heard someone coming around the building. It was the sheriff and his deputies. Lorelei went with them inside and explained the whole situation. About twenty minutes later, forensics showed up and started to go over the place.

About two hours later, the body was taken and the techs went off to examine their findings. The sheriff had already left after telling us to take the scene.

Lorelei called to Warren and said to step up the search for Spadero. Get the Clark County Sheriffs involved too. She hung up and said, "Let's get out of here. Nothing more to find."

We drove back in silence, each with our own thoughts. We got back to the precinct and I told her I was going to my office. I went to my car and drove to the office.

Lacey was talking to some woman at the counter when I came in.

"Jim, good timing. This woman would like to talk to you. About the Isham case."

"Okay, please follow me," I said and took her to my office. She looked familiar, maybe from the restaurant last night. I asked her to sit, she did. "You are?"

"Lisa Donner, I was a good friend of Percy."

"Okay, what can I do for you?"

She was silent for a moment, then said, "I lied last night. I feel bad so I want to make up for it now."

"Okay, what do you want to correct?"

"I know who the killer is. The one who killed Percy."

"How do you know this?" I sat up and paid attention.

"I was in Isham's office the night he was killed. I was coming in to talk to him and I heard the gun shot. I was in the hallway when the killer came out. He didn't see me. I went in to Percy's office and saw him on the floor, then I ran. I was afraid for my life. Can you protect me?"

"Of course. Now who did you see?"

She paused for a moment. I gave her the time to gather her bravery up.

"I'll be sure to have you protected. Talk to me."

She looked around, then said quietly, "It was Doctor Moor."

*

Chapter 29

That information hit me. Now I was confused as to why Yellen was murdered. "You actually saw Moor shoot Isham?"

"No. As I said, I was in the hallway and heard talking, then the gunshot. Moor came out of the office and left. I went in and found Percy on the floor in his blood. I was frightened that Moor might come back so I left quickly. I was scared to tell anyone."

"You heard talking. What did you hear?"

"I heard Percy tell Moor to leave or he'd call the police. Moor said he wanted the money Percy had hidden or he would kill him. I didn't see what happened then, but I heard the gun fire and then Moor left."

"Okay, let me call a friend on the LV police and get you protection. Then you'll have to explain everything to her," I said.

"Is this the same woman cop from last night?" she asked.

"Yes, it is. Detective Paris. She's good people and will help you." I reached for my phone and called Lorelei. She came on and I said she should get to my office quickly. "I have a witness to Isham's murder."

Fifteen minutes later Lorelei and Warren were in my office. We all sat as Lisa repeated her story. Lorelei sat back and smiled.

"That SOB. He lied to us all this time." Lorelei turned back to Lisa. "What was Moor like when he was at the parties?"

"Moor is gay. He and Yellen were partners so they never participated in the party. They just liked to watch. It was creepy."

"Well, he told the truth about watching," I said to Lorelei.

Warren asked, "You want me to have Moor pulled in?"

"No, not yet. He doesn't know we know. I think we should pay him a visit first. Call for a car to take Miss Donner in to get her statement on file. Record everything she says. Have Williams do that, you come with us to Moor's."

Warren went out of the room to call. Lorelei expressed to Lisa her appreciation for coming forth with the info.

"I was starting to feel real bad about Percy' death, and everyone was blaming him for the AIDS stuff. He wasn't killed because of that. It was his money. Why would Moor need money?"

Network Murders

"Moor told me that Yellen had a gambling problem, but I'm wondering if it was Moor who had the problem," Lorelei said. "But why was Yellen murdered?"

"Maybe we'll find out when we talk to Moor," I said.

We waited for the officer to come for Lisa, then we got ready to go find Moor. Lorelei called the hospital and was told Moor was at his office today on Rancho. She got the address and we went out to my car this time. No way was I going to squeeze into the Mustang with Warren.

We drove out, found the building and sat in the parking lot for a few minutes. "I think I will call for a car to come by. Just in case. A couple uniforms will make it official." She made a call to dispatch and we waited for the patrol car to arrive.

She explained what she wanted them to do, hang back until she called. We went in the building and over to the receptionist.

Lorelei flashed her badge and said, "Which office is Doctor Moor in, please?"

The girl said she'd announce us. "Don't even pick up that phone. Where is Moor right now?" she demanded.

The girl pointed to a door and said, "He has someone in with him."

"Fine, we'll see ourselves in." We went to the door and Lorelei opened it.

Moor was at his desk facing us and there was a man in a chair facing Moor. We couldn't see his face. Lorelei went in first, followed by Warren. I held back just outside the door. Moor looked shocked to see us and stood. The man in the chair stood, went to the side of the desk and turned. It was Tommy Spadero.

Lorelei brought her weapon out as did Warren. I had my Glock in hand but I stayed outside the room next to the door. Spadero moved around to Moor and grabbed him, pulling his gun and holding it to Moor's head.

"Back off, cops, or he's dead!" Spadero barked.

"You'd be doing us a favor," Lorelei said. "He murdered Isham, so he's going to be put away. You kill him, it will save the county lots of money in room and board."

Spadero looked confused. "What the hell you talking about? Yellen killed Isham for his money."

"We have a witness who was in the office the night Moor killed Isham. Why do you believe Yellen killed Isham?"

"Moor told me. He said Yellen had gotten into the safe and took the money. It was gone when I got to Isham's house. I went to find Yellen and he said he didn't have the money so I shot him. You telling me this weasel has the money?"

Moor looked frantic and said, "Tommy, they're lying to you. Yellen had the cash, all of it. He called me saying

215

he was leaving Las Vegas and going somewhere safe. I'm telling you the truth."

"Maybe I will plug you for bringing me into this mess. You said we'd split the money and we'd all be rich. Now you had me kill Yellen and you were probably planning to kill me too," Spadero said and cocked the gun.

"Don't do it, Spadero!" Lorelei yelled. "You shoot him, you know we'll shoot you!"

Spadero pulled Moor around the desk and towards the door. Lorelei and Warren backed out of the room. I was on the side of the door where Spadero couldn't see me. Lorelei and Warren moved to the center of the room. The receptionist saw what was happening and ran out of the room.

I was watching for Moor and Spadero to exit as I held my Glock up. Moor came through the door first then Spadero. They moved towards Lorelei and I came up behind Spadero, put my Glock into the back of his neck and said quietly, "Make me pull the trigger."

Spadero held his gun up and Lorelei came over to grab it. Moor ran to the other side of the room. Warren came over and yanked Spadero around to put the cuffs on him.

Lorelei smiled at me. "I guess you're good for something."

"Now you sound like my wife," I said with a grin. I looked at Moor as he headed for the exit. He pulled the door open and started to go out, but the two uniforms standing just outside stopped him.

"Good thing you called for backup," Warren said to her.

Two hours later we had Moor and Spadero in separate interrogation rooms. Spadero was handcuffed to the table. We didn't trust him. Spadero was the most talkative.

"Moor got me involved to break into the safe. I have experience. He said Yellen found out about the money and was going to take care of Isham and get a key to Isham's home. I went to the condo and found the safe already open. I went back to Moor and he said Yellen was double-crossing us and gave me his address out in Lake Mead. I went there and Yellen denied everything. I got a little mad and killed him. Why not? He was lying and double-crossing us. Moor said he didn't know what Yellen did with the money. That's when you came into his office."

"Just how much was in Isham's safe?" Lorelei asked.

"I was told over one million dollars. That's what Moor told me. I never saw the money. I guess Moor has it somewhere."

"We'll find it. Now write this all down." She pushed the pad towards him. She turned to me where I sat by the door and said, "Let's go beat on Moor a little." She told Warren to watch Spadero and we went out.

In the other interrogation room Moor sat patiently waiting. We watched him through the magic mirror from observation as he fidgeted. "To look at him you wonder how he could have come up with this."

"Yep, not very menacing is he?" I said.

"Let's go talk," she said and we went to the other room. Moor jumped as we came in, but said nothing.

"Moor, we got you for the murder of Isham. Spadero admitted to killing Yellen, but I presume you murdered Candy Cane for the key," Lorelei said.

He sat there looking stupid.

"We know you have the money, but where you hid it, that's another matter," I said.

"And you'll never find it. That's my secret now," Moor said. "I'm not admitting to anything about the murders. You can't prove it and your witness is lying. Yellen killed Isham."

"Well, while we were waiting here, I had a team go search your apartment and they found a gun. The same caliber as that which killed Isham. I'm sure tests will prove it to be the gun and probably have your prints on it. You're not very bright. We don't have much to talk to you about. We just would like to know where you hid the money."

"Don't hold your breath waiting," he said and sat back.

"Okay, nothing more to do other than arraign you and get a trial for murder. Hope you fry," Lorelei said and stood. I followed her out of the room. We stood in the squad room as Moor was taken back to his cell.

"With Isham gone and no relatives, the money is now open to whoever finds it," I said.

"Are you going to go look for it?" Lorelei asked.

"I'd be crazy not to," I said with a grin.

*

Chapter 30

We spent the next day with Angelo, Sophia and Frances having a picnic in our backyard. Frances was heading back to New York in two days and we wanted to spend a little time before she left. We had a nice visit and then our company left.

Penny and I sat in the living room resting. Willy was sleeping on the couch next to Penny.

"So the money is still missing?" she asked.

"Yep, unless Moor tells us, it's not going to be found easily. I'm sure someone will find it unless he hid it well. I'm not going to bother. If it does get found the police will confiscate it as evidence in Isham's murder. So I'm not killing myself. Lorelei found out that Isham had no relatives, so the money would be held until someone can legally claim it. Too bad."

Network Murders

"Did you talk to Wallace Glass about solving the case?"

"Yes, I did. And he cut a check for a handsome sum. He was happy that the murder didn't have anything to do with your show," I said.

"I'm glad too. What ever happened to that cop you said was working for the bookies?"

"He finally confessed and IAB is going to charge him with the attempted murder of Buzz Lightyear. Buzz has identified him as threatening Isham. Turns out Isham was providing drugs to his guests and not paying the dealers. He was lucky they didn't kill him."

"Yeah, lucky to get murdered by a doctor."

"We still don't know how Moor got into the safe. He's not talking."

"Maybe he hired a safe cracker and paid him off to keep quiet," Penny said.

"Very true, good deduction. I'll mention that to Lorelei."

Someone knocked on our front door causing me to jump. "Why didn't the drive alarm go off?" I said.

"Because you didn't reset it after Angelo left," she said.

I stood and went to the door, peeking through the peep hole. It was Lynn, Deacon and baby. I told Penny and she jumped up and came to the door.

I opened it and said, "Hey, guys, welcome. You couldn't call first?"

"We wanted to surprise you two," Lynn said as they came in.

Penny was going crazy over the baby. Lynn handed her to Penny. She took the baby to the couch.

"Come and sit. Angelo, his mother and his girlfriend just left," I said.

"Girlfriend? Angelo has a girlfriend?" Deacon asked.

"Yes, he does. Sit and I'll tell you about her," I said.

They sat and we explained the whole story about the new lady in Angelo's life.

After I finished, Lynn sat forward on the couch and said, "Jim, Deacon and I have had a serious talk and I decided to take you up on your offer to work part-time in your firm," Lynn said. "I want to start part-time for now and see how it goes. I'm tired of police work, but I need to keep busy. You seem to fall into the good crimes so I may be able to keep my hands in it but with no pressure from people like Weber or the chief."

"Well, I'm happy to welcome you to the team. We'll have to get everyone together and have a party. When do you want to start?"

"Anytime you say. The baby is getting big enough to be with a sitter. I talked to Paula and she is ready to do it. Earl will have to get used to having a baby around. He'll get over it," she said with a laugh.

"This is great. You'll be an asset to the team. Let's say next Monday to start. That will give you a few days to organize. You may have to share an office or we'll have to add on to the building."

"No problem, you can put me in with Trapper. He gets along fine with me."

"Actually, I have the biggest office and I'm hardly ever in, so you can share with me."

"Whatever you say, boss," she said with a grin.

"We'll work it out," I said as my phone buzzed. I excused myself and went to the kitchen.

The caller ID said private, but I answered. "Hello?"

"Mr. Richards?" came a female voice.

"Yes, I am. Who's this?"

"Who I am is not important. I just have a question."

"Okay, ask."

"What would happen if the money that Moor hid was found?"

"Well, it would be evidence in the murder case, then someone legitimate would have to claim it," I said.

"Legitimate? As in?"

"Related to Isham by blood or by marriage."

She was silent for a moment. I asked, "Have you found the money?"

She didn't answer right away, then said, "Yes, but I'm not keeping it all. Just enough to take my son and get away from Vegas to start over. I gave part of it to the homeless shelter agency and then a couple of churches that have soup kitchens. I gave most of it to the abused spouse agency and shelter in town. They were a big help to me in the past. I hope I'm not going to get in trouble."

"Well, I'm sure the police would have liked to get it back, but I won't tell. Where did you find it?"

"In his office, in a secret compartment he had in his closet."

I thought it was probably his receptionist, but I didn't ask. "Did you know about this compartment? Or just hunt around?"

"I knew it was there. I caught him in it once before," she said. "I'm saying too much. I just wanted to tell you that the money has been found and put to good use to help those in need. Moor didn't care about anyone other than himself."

"Well, good luck to you and your son. I hope you have a good life and I'm sure the people you helped will be very thankful. That was a good thing you did."

"Thank you," she said and then hung up.

I went back out to our friends and sat. Penny looked at me and asked, "Who was it?"

"An angel. I'll explain later," I said and smiled.

*

THE END

For every ending there's a new beginning.

Bob Moats

Here's a free preview of the next book, "Reunion Murders"

Chapter 1

The man hobbled down the stairs, slowly taking one step at a time. His leg was aching from his childhood injuries that now developed into arthritis. He hated getting old. He ambled to the door on the side of the basement, and with a key from his wallet he unlocked the door. He went in and over to the desk that sat along one wall, turning on the desk light. He picked up his prescription bottle and popped out a couple pills that the doctors told him would ease the pain. He opened the bottle of whiskey from a shelf and downed a shot glass of the liquid to wash down the pills.

He turned to the wall opposite the desk and went to it. He turned on another light, brightening a corkboard filled with photos. He stood, examining one particular photo of people grouped in the center. One woman and two men were of his interest.

He got closer to study them. Then, he pulled out a thin knife and started to stab the people in the photo, one at a time. One after another, right through their bodies, close to the heart.

"Soon, I will be stabbing you in the hearts," he said to the photo.

~~*~~

225

Network Murders

The invitation was addressed to the home of Jim Richards and his wife Penny Wickens.

Penny was not home when the mail came. She was interviewing guests on her TV show in Vegas. It was on a network station broadcasting across the country. I was feeding our dog, Willy, a toy Yorkie we've had for a number years since before we moved to Vegas from Michigan.

I jumped when I heard an alarm go off. It was a security feature that came with the house we purchased when we first moved to Vegas. I liked the security features of the house and Penny liked the stripper pole planted out by the half-sized Olympic pool out back. The house sat on a lonely road overlooking the Las Vegas valley and the strip of casinos and hotels in the distance. It was also at the foot of one of the mountains that ranged around the valley affording us privacy from the back of our property.

I shut down the alarm, turned on the monitor and saw it was a postal worker driving away in the truck. I took Willy out for a walk and a dump as I went to the mail box on a post by the road. Willy chased a butterfly while I took the mail out of the box.

"Willy, stop!" I yelled to the dog before he could catch the butterfly. Willy stopped and sat down, looking at me with his dumb expression. "Good puppy," I said and walked back to the house. Willy followed.

Bob Moats

At the snack bar I looked over the mail. Mostly junk wanting us to sign up for some credit card or for car insurance. I sorted and tossed the junk. Then, I studied one envelope, a square beige greeting card sized envelope addressed to us with very neat script handwriting. It was stamped with a forwarding address from our old address in Michigan. I was amazed it took almost six months to get to us.

I carefully opened the envelope and pulled a card out. It was an engraved invitation from Penny's and my old high school back in Michigan. It was for a class reunion.

I tried to do the math in my head, I still couldn't. The invite said it was a forty-five year reunion but I felt that was short by a year or two. I wondered if Penny would want to go back to Michigan to this reunion. The invite said that due to problems, the reunion last year, number forty-five had been canceled. So they were backing up one year.

I smiled. My school always did what they wanted, even changing years. My mind wandered back to just before I met Penny again, after nearly forty years of being away from her. We were in the same school and, although she was a couple years younger than I, she had a really big crush on me. I could never figure out why, but I didn't question it.

My mind also thought about the murders of cheerleaders that took place and Penny was supposed to be one of the victims. That was when Penny and I got back together, much to my delight. We stayed together and then moved out here. Happily ever after. Until I could be murdered by some criminal that I was hired to follow.

227

Network Murders

My private investigating and security firm was thriving, and going through many changes. I sat at the snack bar and set the invite down. Memories were flooding into my head. Some I'd rather forget. We had a good life in Vegas and my firm was keeping me and my associates busy. Will Trapper and Earl Daws, both retired cops from back home in Michigan, joined me at my firm and we picked up a number of people along the way.

Recently, we had a female homicide lieutenant from Vegas LVMPD join our firm. Lynn Carter had retired from the force after she had a baby. My friend and the cop who saved Penny's life, Deacon DeAngelo married Lynn and then they had a beautiful baby girl. I could never remember her full name so I just called her PJ, after Penny and me, which was part of her name.

I picked up my cell phone from where I left it on the counter and called Lacey, my office manager and certifiable crazy person. She picked up after two rings. Long enough for her to see the caller ID.

"If you say you aren't coming in, I'll hunt you down," she said briskly.

"I'm coming in. I just wanted to ask if Penny was there."

"She came in about a half hour ago, after she finished her show for the day."

"She's still there?"

"She is. And wondering where you are."

"I'll be there shortly," I said, and hung up.

I gathered up Willy in his travel pouch and headed out to the Crown Vic. I knew Lynn was coming in today to get settled into her office. Actually, it was my office, but it was big enough for two people and we had no more available room since Buck took the last space for an office. Buck was settling into his duties as a P.I, since his license came in the mail. He was happy and we kept him busy with small cases for now.

I parked and went in the back door. Down the hall, I could see Penny and Lynn talking outside my office door. They both smiled at me as I came up.

"About time you got in. Lynn was ready to throw out all your stuff and take over," Penny said and kissed me on the cheek.

"Morning, Lynn. All moved in I see."

"Yep, ready to start. I applied this morning for my private license, it should be in anytime. Captain Weber wasn't happy that I was leaving the force, but he'll get over it. I feel sorry for Deacon, now alone with Weber. He'll get over it, too. I feel so relaxed being away from the grind of homicide."

"I'll see if we can stir up a murder or two for you," I said with a smile.

"That's all right. I'll take a good embezzlement case, missing person or even follow a cheating spouse."

Network Murders

"Oh, I have some mail you might like to see," I said to Penny as I let Willy out of his bag and pulled the invitation from the front pouch, handing it to her.

She opened it and read the card, smiling. "So, we have to go back to Michigan for this?"

"We could fly everyone out here for the thing. But, I don't feel like putting out that much money to see people I hardly knew in high school," I said.

"It would be interesting to go back and see the people we couldn't stand. Maybe I'll see a few friends and we can visit with your family. We haven't seen them in a few years."

"True. This letter was delayed because of our move, so we have one week to get all pretty to go show off for everyone. Shall I R.S.V.P. our visit?"

"Go ahead. I'm game to show you off now that you're a famous private dick," Penny said laughing.

Lynn said, "Sure, hire me then take off, leaving me alone."

"Don't fret. Jim is hardly in the office anyway. It's almost like you'll be alone a lot," Penny said.

"Hey, I work hard here, too." I defended myself.

"Can't prove it by me," came a voice behind me, it was Lacey. "And who are you?"

"The person who pays you and can fire you," I said with a grin.

*

To find out more about the Jim and Penny books visit murdernovels.com and see what is available.

~~*~~

Jim Richards Family of Readers

Thanks to the following people who are now part of the Jim Richards Family of Readers. They have read a book or more and enjoyed them. They all volunteered to be included in the list. If you are a fan of the books, send me your full name and you will be included in future books. Send your name to murdernovels@bobmoats.com to be added here and on the website.

* Achim Feifel * Al Norris * Alex Wheatley * Alexandra Delporte-Wilkinson * Amy Tapia * Andrea Bryan * Anne Shepherd * Arianda Sugar * Arlene Markowski * Ashley Augustus * Audra Hall * Barbara Hughes * Barbara Sammons * Barbara Schuler * Barbara Zirger * Beth Donohue Plenskofski * Betsy Childress * Beth Gibson * Bill Sandy * Bill Tornquist * Billie-jo Collie * Boni J Rychener * Carl Bishopric * Carla

Network Murders

Lewis * Carole Henderson * Carolyn Conroy * Carolyn Riddle-Linington * Cassy Bailey * Cathie Turner * Chad Hudson * Charlotte L Duran * Cheryl L. Everett * Cindy Ackley Nunn * Cindy Valstad * Connie Bancroft * Corinne Kay O'Daniel * Dana Robbins Chuchran * Dana Wichita * Danielle Monique * Darren Heald * Dave Travers * David Wilkinson * DeAnn Jannereth * Deanna Miller * Deb Breuker Balbo * Debbie Carter * Debbie White * Deborah Fartuch * Deborah Gauze * Deborah Sullivan * Dee King * Denise Freeman * Diana Carver * Dixie Beck * Donna Gould * Donna Thompson * Donny Minter * Doris Kight * Eddie Moore * Eric Walters * Felicia Annette Bradfield * Francine Menor * Gail Chesney * Georgiann Minster * George Conner * Greg Colucci * Hayley Rankin * Harold Garcia * Heidi Arnold * Irma Ranee Coy * Jacqueline Moss * Jan Kimball * Janice Schneider * Janice Spoor * Jennifer Redmond * Jessica Keown-Belous * Jim Beck * Jo Boguslaw * Jo Turner * Joanne Marie Turner * John Peiffer * John Wisbiski * Joseph Wauro * Joyce Stacy * Joyce Trifiletti * Judy Franklin * Judy Travers * Judy Padgett * Julie Heath * Junnahvee Benson * Karen Dahl * Karen Grams * Karen Higham * Karen Kaiser * Karen Meinburg Richwine * Karen Kirkman Parker * Karin Hawkins * Karin Vasvari * Kathleen Donohue Roesing * Kathleen Riddle-Wolfe * Kathy Hinds Moore * Kathy Jones * Kathy Mitchell * Katie Benzler * Kay Burns * Kelly Garcia * Ken Boggs * Keota Rodriguez * Kiera Mccarthy * Kim Estes * Kitty Stolle * Kristie Sciler * Kirsty Stanton * LaLonnie Scallen * Larry Morris * Leann Parr * Lenora Scales * Leslie Marie Jackson * Linda Forester * Linda Ingle Cox * Linda Kennerö * Linda Magill * Lisa Bower * Liz Gibson * Lorraine Wiman * Loretta Alexander * Lynda Bowles * Lynette Lawrance * LuAnn Louttit * Manny Rothman * Marcia Gibson DeWitt * Marie Calder * Marlene Bryan * MaryLouise Kramp * Mary Lynn Gross * Megan Atkins * Meghan Hyden * Melody Cannavan * Michael Carruthers * Michael Dinkens * Michael Vannoy * Michelle Burns-Mitchell * Michelle Pilcher * Micki Potter * Mike Moats * Mimi Baur * Myrna Hecht * Nadine Sutton * Nancy Ellen Sayre * Natalie Quine * Neena Martin * O'Della Wilson * Pat Pollington * Pat

Bob Moats

Rohn * Patricia Jarmon * Patricia C Trezza * Patrick Barry *
Paul Lawrance * Peggy Davis * Phyllis Bassett * Raylene
Matheny * Rebecca Collins Besner * Renee Brumley * Reta
Hanna * Reta Moats * Roberta Navarro-Harder * Sally
Berneathy * Sally Hubler * Sarah Santos * Satka Nikc * Sharon
E. Edwards * Sharon Mangini * Sharon McMillon * Sheena
Rawl * Sherry Amstutz * Shirley Alvarez * Shirley Davies *
Shirley Williams * Stacie Rowe * Stephanie Conner * Steve
Cullen * Susan Haughton * Susan Hesse Adams * Susan
Salomon * Suzan K Chase * Taisha Cullum * Tamara Moore *
Tammy Castleberry * Tammy Lynn Wood * Ted Murphy *
Terri Atkins * Terri Creech * Terry Raab * Tonia Rachael
Riggs-Williams * Travis Fleury-Lopez * Twyla Gawlas * Val
Brooks * Walt Munsel * Yvonne Isakson *

Thank you to all these wonderful people.

Thank you for purchasing this book. I hope
you enjoy it as much as I enjoyed writing it
for my faithful readers. Please feel free to
email me to tell me what you thought about
my stories. I love hearing from the readers. I
can be reached at murdernovels@bobmoats.com
thanks again!